For the Love of *January*

Jackie Clark

Published by: Wendiilou Publishing
                        Wendy Brown

Cover by: 

For more copies, contact the publisher c/-
212 Glenburnie Rd
Rob Roy NSW 2360
wendiiloupublishing@gmail.com
0468 998 268

Please note: This book has been written and published in Australia, and as such, Australian spelling conventions have been used throughout.

Dedication.

This book is dedicated to my Poppa. Of all the people in my life, he was the one who was always there for me, no matter what, even at 3am, if I needed help, he would get in the car and come get me. He was a true blue, one of a kind larakin, who could fix aka "MacGyver" anything with a roll of duct tape and 100 screws... He was an avid reader, large print of course lol... and I know he would be bloody proud of me and these stories.

For the Love of
January

Chapter 1

The black and white semi-trailer, loaded with hay bales, was parked at the truck stop in the central Western Australian town of Cannondale, it was the well-known last fuel stop for 500 kilometres then nothing but a stretch of highway through the middle of Australia that never seemed to turn. The rain was relentless that evening, filling the grooves in the road and leaving a misty sheen hanging in the air above the puddles before settling again after each wheel passed through it.

Abby hid behind a skip bin at the back of the car park watching the drivers parking their rigs then going in for dinner. The lights across the open car park were dull, leaving her to pass through the shadowed areas easily undetected.

It took her nearly twelve months to plan leaving Rick, her abusive partner. She worked at the truck stop he owned during the day, and he was at home with her most nights, so she was never too far from his reach. The cleaner, Rosanna, didn't speak much English, but they had built a bond over the years. She was from the Dominican Republic, she may not have understood a lot of English, but she understood enough to see what was happening, agreeing to help her hide what she needed. A backpack hidden in the bottom of the female toilet's sanitary garbage bin. Each week they added to a zip lock bag of mostly five and ten-dollar notes and gold coins. It was convenient to take a small amount from the tipping jar, or when customers said to keep the change, when she was working, without him noticing, putting it in the bag when she went to the toilet. Over the space of 11 months, Rosanna helped her add to the contents, it was easy to keep it hidden in the ladies' toilets, not many men would want to check the sanitary product waste bin, Rosanna was the only one who cleaned and changed it. They added a variety of prepaid items, such as supermarket gift cards and a phone, that were purchased in town by Rosanna so not to attract attention. Rosanna also added her phone number under the guise Ross River Vets to the prepaid phone so once she had left, she could keep in contact in case he ever set out to find her. The days went along like normal. Abby worked her shifts as normal; she did the best she could to do as she was told and keep him happy. She knew the time would eventually come when a chance would present itself. It was a game of life, a deadly game, if she got caught it was over, no second chances, only one chance which she had to be ready for.

The house and truck stop were full of cameras. He had, had her trapped there since she was 19, she hardly remembered what it was like to not be constantly ridiculed or watched, never leaving her alone for too long, if he did, she was locked in the bedroom. He was violent, degrading, and believed in his mind that she was his property. He got angry easily, of course it was always her fault, he had bashed her, broken bones, even nearly killing her once, she saved herself because she managed to talk him down, much like the way she had to talk one of her foster dads down when he had drunk too much. He never used to be like this. When she first met him, he was charming and kind. After the first year he began to change.

 In a strange reality she couldn't tell anyone about what was going on, everyone liked him, he had the persona of a friendly all-round nice guy, always helping others and had a good reputation amongst the community, no one suspected the hell she lived in even when she had bruises on her face or a broken arm. She knew it wasn't going to be easy to hide from him locally, she had to disappear completely without a trace.

Every Wednesday he would do a night shift leaving her home with the bedroom door locked from the outside, the window was nailed shut from the outside so there was absolutely no chance to easily escape. His routine was the same every time which made her planning even harder, but this time it was different. Lightning lit up the sky every few minutes and the heavy rain had made their yard and driveway so muddy he bogged the car. He came upstairs and looked in the room. She lay in bed, her eyes closed, laying as still as she could, pretending to sleep, even snoring a little. He seemed to watch her for a while, she didn't move, kept the composure, when he was agitated, he would lash out, she prayed that he would not this time. She listened to him go back down the stairs and out the front door, he furiously threw things against the side of the house and swore trying to get the small sedan out without success. She heard the old motorbike engine start and slowly the sound of its motor got quieter as he got further away.

This was the moment, the chance she had needed, for this time he didn't follow his routine, he was so angry and distracted, she didn't remember hearing the noise the slide bolt made as he locked the door. Abby's heart raced. She slowly got out of bed and walked towards the bedroom door. Turning the handle carefully, taking a deep breath pushed the door open. Abby quickly pulled on a pair of jeans, runners, a black hoodie and coat. She quickly made her way down the stairs. She pressed her body against the wall at the base. There was a motion detector on the wall. She waited patiently for the lightning before moving past it. The lightning had sometimes set the detectors off in the past so she knew Rick would probably ignore the alarm. It was a risk she was willing to take, she was already further than she could have dreamed of getting.

The bag was at the truck stop, where he was. The darkness, combined with the rain, offered her a shield from being seen. She walked the three blocks to the truck stop, sticking close to the residents' fences and stopping motionless against trees whenever a car came past. The toilets were on the outside of the building near a line of wheelie bins. She crouched behind the small brick wall that surrounded the open bitumen area where the trucks parked. She crawled along under three trailers. She could see Rick through the window sitting at the front counter on his phone and in front of the security camera monitors. The toilet doors only had one camera, luckily for her it had been knocked out of alignment by a pigeon and he had not fixed it. The toilet doors were usually unlocked around dinner time, it would make him angry with people asking for the keys all the time. If he turned in his chair the right way, he could see the doors from where he sat. Lightning struck again, he stood up and walked across the store and looked out the front double doors towards the strike. This was it, she ran out from under the trailer and into the darkness, as she clasped the toilet door handle, it unlatched, and she pushed it open and once again all was silent as she stood soaking wet in the vacant ladies' toilet. Abby pulled the lid free from the bin pulling out the garbage bag to see her backpack, it was still there. The sense of urgency that crept over her now was suffocating. At any moment someone or even Rick could walk in that door, and it would all be over. She looked in the tiny bathroom mirror, taking the scissors from the bag she cut off her long hair, hiding the pieces in a sanitary bag, sliding it back in replacing the lid. Abby put on the black baseball cap from the bag, tucking her now shoulder length brown hair up under it to try and disguise herself. Standing at the door, she paused, looking back at the room, everything looked normal, her fingers squeezed the handle tightly as she edged the door open. Keeping her head down and back to the wall she edged herself out and crouched behind the skip bin at the edge of the building. He was sitting back at the counter serving a man.

The black and white rig was the only one left, no driver in sight. The rain started falling heavier. It fell like a wall of water, she could barely see the trailer ten meters in front of her, which meant the chances of him seeing her were low, she waited for the next lightning strike in case then she ran across. The plastic wrapped hay bales were tied down tight across the top with a large cover to protect the load. Abby unlooped the corner of the cover to look under, there was a gap between the bales that went from one side to another leaving a half meter wide crawl space in the middle where some of the bales had been removed. She looked around again to make sure no one was around before pulling herself up the side and into the space between the bales. She pushed the rope back through the loop along the edge of the trailer and pulled it down tight using a variety of messy knots.

She sat between the bales quietly. She glanced at her watch, 10.37pm. It would be at least 6 hours before Rick would go home, that was 6 hours head start. He would come after her, he had threatened it many times if she ever tried to leave. Looking above her the bales were stacked 3 high. After another four lightning strikes, she felt the truck's engine vibrate as it started up. Slowly the semi drove across the car park and turned left out onto the highway. For now, she was free, after nearly a year playing the game, trying to keep him happy and herself safe, Abby took a deep, freedom-filled breath.

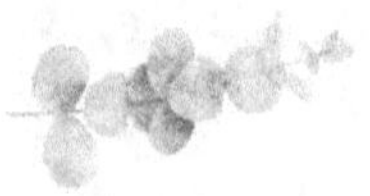

Abby opened her eyes, the constant, comforting vibration of the truck's engine had stopped. It was now daytime. She looked at her watch, it read 9.40am. that's over 10 hours since she left. By now Rick would have been home and found her gone. She put her backpack on and tucked her hair back into her cap. She had no idea where she was. She could hear cars passing constantly so knew she was in a town. She crawled along the length of the truck and carefully undid the bunch of mismatched knots she tied the night before. She looked out of the hole between the bales. She was on the side of the road outside a shopping center. She jumped down and walked quickly towards the plaza. Looking around she read the signs and street names. She was in Woodend. She was still in Western Australia. Abby felt nervous. Walking into the plaza she found the bathrooms. She locked herself in the parent's room toilets. Abby took off the baseball cap, hoodie and coat and dropped them into the garbage. She wore the same tank top and jeans. Running some water over her hands and through her hair she still had enough length to put it up in a low ponytail.

So many things ran through her mind, she wasn't far enough away to feel completely at ease. Now she felt like she stood out to everyone around her, not having anything but the clothes on her back and the backpack, it was time to go shopping. Abby needed to blend in. She used the gift voucher to Target that was in the zip lock bag. She bought clothes, shoes, toiletries, a wallet, and a handheld duffle bag.

Heading back to the bathrooms she packed the bag with her newly purchased clothes. Took off the ones she had on also leaving them in the garbage bin. In her mind she had to completely leave the life with Rick behind and that meant the clothes she wore. She turned on the mobile phone for the first time, it let out a few notifications, all from Ross River Vets.

"Come to pay bill, you gone". Rosanna wasn't great with her English, but she understood, keeping with the idea that it was the vets she was talking to in fear of being discovered there were three more text messages.

"Very mad, cat ran way, looking everywhere". Abby knew what was going to happen next, she just hoped she had been prepared enough.

"Vet closed few days, gone to find cat". Abby tucked the phone into her handbag, putting the money and cards into the wallet she purchased she looked into the mirror. She wore a black pair of jeans and boots, a long sleeve shirt and knee length cardigan. Introducing herself now as Katie Thompson she stepped into her new identity. Where Rosanna got her a driver's license or bank account and cards with her new name on it, she wasn't game to ask, but she was thankful.

Katie waited patiently at the train station. The ticket in her hand was to Melbourne. She didn't really have a plan, just to get as far away as possible, everything from this point onwards was new, exciting, but terrifying at the same time.

Chapter 2

Katie stepped off the train in Melbourne, she was 22 and had never been to the city before, the tall skyscrapers took her breath away and, like any tourist, she spent a lot of her time looking up. Katie had thought a lot about what her next move would be. She knew she had to get as far away as possible. Catching the bus to Geelong, she arrived late in the afternoon ready to board the Spirit of Tasmania across to Tassie. Those times she had been working at the truck stop, helping out in the kitchen gave her a lot of time to watch tv, the television was on 24/7 in the dining room for the truckies to watch, although it had usually only been on sports channels, she once saw a small town in Tasmania called Eaglehawk Neck on a travel show that was so beautiful it always stuck in her mind as being where she would go.

There were no new text messages from Rosanna which gave her an edge of confidence and she started to relax a bit. The Spirit of Tasmania was a large ship, capable of carrying 500 cars and 1400 passengers across from mainland Australia to Tasmania. She boarded the overnight sail.

Her cabin was small and had two single beds either side of a porthole window looking out onto the ocean. Her bag sat neatly on the bedside table. Standing in the steaming, hot shower, the sense of freedom felt more real. She still felt scared though and ordered her dinner to be delivered to her cabin. So many thoughts ran across her mind as she lay in the single bed that night. Making lists in her mind of what she needed to do, she slowly drifted off to sleep.

The ship pulled into Devenport early the next morning. The fog sat heavily in the air as she walked out of the terminal, catching a taxi into the centre of the city to central station. Katie booked a bus to Eaglehawk Neck, it was 242kms. In 242kms she would have come to the end of her journey, she patiently sat in the waiting room for the bus to arrive. There was a small café in the station. She bought a small tray of sandwiches and a bottle of water. It started raining when she boarded the bus. The seats were comfortable, it was the kind of bus that had a toilet at the back and there were only 5 passengers. Her seat was a window seat. She checked her phone. No messages. Katie wasn't sure if that was a good thing or not, it made her nervous. She knew for sure he would be looking for her, he was the type that wouldn't give up easy. There was nothing at the truck stop or the house that would indicate where she went. Rick had no idea which direction she went, how or exactly when she left. Katie had the upper hand. She tried to pull her thoughts back to moving in a forward direction. Unfolding the list she made on the ship, she read over the points. Accommodation, job, car. Looking around the bus checking if anyone was watching she opened her wallet, unzipping the side compartment to reveal a blanket of pink and blue. The five- and ten-dollar notes were packed in tightly. She counted the money she had left, just over three thousand dollars.

Watching the countryside change as she got closer to Eaglehawk, Katie let herself relax and she actually started to feel excited.

The bus pulled into the bus stop at the visitor's centre later in the afternoon. Katie stood in the car park with no plan, no idea where or what she was going to do, but this town was what she had longed for ever since she saw it on television. Eaglehawk Neck was, from what she had seen on tv and through the brochures she had picked up from the visitor's centre, a collection of sand dunes about 150 meters wide. Pirate Bay was on one side and Eaglehawk Bay on the other. It was a village, famous for being the point that prevented convicts escaping the Penal colony, Port Arthur, which was only 20kms away. According to the history brochure, during the 1800's to prevent escapees, The Dog Line was established, it was up to 9 vicious dogs with old barrels as kennels, close enough to each other to barely touch but not close enough to fight. Oil Lamps were dotted along the dog line, scattered cockle shells were used on the ground to reflect the light. She noticed a bronze statue near the community hall of a large dog and oil lamp in remembrance of the town's rich history. Most of the foreshore was now a coastal reserve.

Katie made her way to The Lufra Hotel, the same one as she had seen on the travel show. The view of Pirates Bay from the verandah, the deep blue colour of the ocean, was soothing to the soul. Louise, the owner, was sitting at the reception desk, she was lovely and more than helpful with making her feel at home. She filled out the check in form, pausing to make sure the name she wrote was correct. She paid in cash, booking for the week in one of the self-contained apartments the hotel had to offer. It was a start anyway to her new life. What happened after that she would leave to chance.

She pushed the key into the door. Standing there for a moment she took a deep breath and turned the key, the door easily opened. The apartment was 2 stories. The ground level had a beautiful, coastal theme lounge room and kitchen, leading upstairs into a large bedroom with king size bed and ensuite bathroom. Katie began to cry; she couldn't control it. She had never had her own place and felt overwhelmed by how breathtaking the apartment was in person. She lay on the bed looking out of the glass doors onto the balcony at the colour changing sky. So many things were running through her mind, so many things she had to do, but for now, in this moment she breathed deeply, feeling completely free.

Chapter 3

Katie startled herself awake, breathing hard, sweating heavily. Looking around she rubbed her eyes and rolled out of bed. Washing her face, looking in the mirror at a messy knot of hair nestled on the top of her head. She laughed at the sight of herself, but it didn't matter, not one bit, she had no one there to tell her she couldn't just stay that way all day. Today she planned to explore her new hometown with an extensive list of places that she saw on the television and wanted to see in person. Katie stepped out of the front door of her apartment, hanging the 'do not clean' sign on the door while pushing the button on the back of the handle to lock it.

The sun was becoming brighter in the very early morning, but the air was cool. Across the road from the hotel was one of the first places on her list, The Tessellated Pavement. According to Louise, the owner of the hotel, the pavement is a naturally occurring phenomenon. The many grooves in the flat surface to her looked like someone has cut them with a saw, in some parts like a big lump of playdough, the sections between the cuts rising up in perfectly rounded lumps. It was hundreds of squares and rectangles all side by side. With the right angle the light hit the water, looking like rice paddies with the water settling in each shape. Katie sat on the wall like border at the side and just watched the water. The sky was pink and yellow as the sun rose higher, reflecting off the pavement squares creating a flat mosaic floor. It really was beautiful and seemed to change colours and shape with every minute that passed by. Sitting there listening to the cars on the road behind her one problem was starting to present itself the more and more she thought about it. EagleHawk and surrounds was scattered amongst wide area of bushland and long stretches of sandy shoreline, it was too far to walk from place to place. Walking back up to The Lufra for breakfast, she pondered ideas of what to do.

"Good morning, Darl, how was your night?", Louise asked as she ate her breakfast.

"It was good thank you, I was hoping if you had a few minutes spare to chat?" Katie asked politely. Louise sat across from her at the table. Katie was so nervous her stomach was churning.

"I was hoping you can let me know of the local bus timetable or a way to get around?". Louise thought about it for a moment. "We have a taxi service but it's just a couple of cars, if you need a car, I have an old run about in the bottom shed you're welcome to use till you get a car".

Katie nearly squealed with joy. "Really? That would be amazing".

"Call by the office after you finish breaky and I'll give you the keys, you will just need to put fuel in it".

Katie pushed up the roller door, it sent out a loud screeching metal on metal echo through the car park that the entire town would surely have heard. It was a Suzuki Jimny, by the look of it, it had been around since the stone age. It was a pale green in colour, with the clear coat peeling off in multiple places. It was a 2 door and had a strangely large, plastic type bull bar attached to the front with a pair of yellow glass fog lights mounted in the middle. The door opened with a slight creak as she climbed into the driver's seat. The interior was original, had a faint smell lingering inside, a mix of dust and cigarettes.

It took a few tries, but she got it started. It had been a while since she drove a manual, the bunny hopping was almost embarrassing. It was mortifying but the most fun she had had in years. She headed her little ride up Pirate's Bay drive into town. Eaglehawk wasn't a big place, it had a few cafés and a small IGA supermarket. Pulling up at The Blowhole carpark she found the Doolishus Food Van and a lady selling freshly picked strawberries. It was one of the places she had seen the presenter go to on the travel show she first saw Eaglehawk Neck on. She waited in line ordering fresh local caught fish and chips. Everyone seemed happy, many tourists by the look of the people and guided groups there were around. Her order number was called, her fish and chips were served in a cone shape paper holder. Something she had never seen before.

"Are you new in town or just visiting?" The lady selling the strawberries asked.

Katie smiled and walked closer to her. She would have been in her 60's and had curly short hair.

"I am new here; does it show that easily?" Katie laughed nervously. The lady stood up and lent over the table extending her hand.

"My name is Dot". Katie shook her hand and introduced herself. "Where have you come from?". Katie felt nervous suddenly.

"Ahh, Western Australia".

Dot walked around to the front of the table to Katie. She could sense the sudden tension and change in her face. "I have lived here for nearly 50 years, if you need anything don't hesitate to ask." Dot touched Katie's arm in a sign of affection and comfort, but she still flinched. Dot looked at her up and down like she could see through her completely.

"Thank you, I'll see you another time". Katie walked quickly back to her little car. She sat in the driver's seat trying to control her breathing, trying to ward away the panic attack that was coming over her. Not everyone was out to get her, not everyone was watching her, even though it felt that way. She ate the chips and calmed herself down. She drove into town to the IGA. Pushing the trolley around she again started to feel anxious. The realization that she was on her own was setting in, it was exhilarating but also scary. Unfolding another list from her wallet she pushed the trolley up and down the aisles. Going through the checkout Katie saw a community noticeboard. There was a listing for a stable hand. She had never seen a horse in real life let alone worked in a stable but there was something about it that felt right. Tearing off the phone number she put it in her pocket and pushed the trolley back into the bay after loading her groceries.

Katie pulled Little Jim, as she now affectionately called the Suzuki bomb, into the parking bay at the front of her apartment and carried the bags inside.

Katie felt scared to call the number, so she texted it instead. Nearly instantly her phone rang with the same number she had texted.

"Hello". Katie nearly melted all over the floor she was so scared to answer.

"G'Day This is Gage Morgan, you sent me a text about the stable hand position". The man's voice was deep and raspy.

"Yes, I did, I don't have any experience though, I am new to town and saw your notice in the supermarket".

"That's ok, I've had no one interested in the position so far, so if you want to pop out for a chat today, I can show you around", he said eagerly. Katie agreed and he gave her directions.

She turned on to Gelling Rd., following the directions he texted her. She drove 3kms down the bitumen before coming to a large dam and wall entry way. The entrance to the property was enormous. On each side were stone walls that looked like the stone had been hand cut, imperfect shapes that fit exactly into place beside the next one. Coming from each wall was a metal archway, unique twisted metal strips shaped into filigree like leaves. The name of the property was grandly on display over the road, she drove across the cattle grid, looking up through the windscreen to read. "Endeavour Park", behind the stone walls it opened up onto a wide gravel road and a vast collection of paddocks, all of them exactly the same size, each small paddock's gate opened up onto the main road she was on. She counted 7 paddocks before the road turned, another 5 paddocks later she came to a large building with Endeavour Park written on the side. She parked

Little Jim and got out to look around. Katie had never been on a horse stud before, nor had she ever seen such a big building. Roller doors at one end with parking bays for horse floats, a big double set of sliding metal doors in the middle, looking down a wide breezeway with smaller indoor stables on each side. It was grand, perfectly manicured gardens and walkways went in several different directions all with neatly painted signs. Katie felt very out of place, her comfort zone was surely being tested big time standing there, every part of her wanted to get back in Little Jim and drive back to town.

"You must be Katie". A gentle, softly spoken young lady said, walking down the breezeway to greet her. "I'm Lily". Katie was taken off guard by the affectionate, blonde teenager as she hugged her tightly. Lily looked about 14, she had neatly braided hair, knee-high boots, tan-coloured jodhpurs, a long sleeve, white shirt and dark brown vest with Endeavour Park embroidered in white on one side.

"Have you ever been on a horse before?"

Katie shook her head nervously which didn't faze Lily who had linked arms with her and led her happily towards the indoor stables. Strangely, this bubbly teenager had her completely at ease, not scared or looking around for people watching, completely present in the moment. She felt happy.

Chapter 4

Lily led Katie down the breezeway. There were 5 stables on each side. Each of the stables were numbered with the horses in residence's name written on the chalk board attached above the door at the front of the stall. Each stall had a set of hooks on the front wall with coloured lead ropes and halters hanging from them. Holding her hand up high, she started on the left, pointing at each stall. This is Barney, Leeroy, Clementine, Marilyn, and Sherlock. Pointing to the right side, Fernando, Dodge, Angel, Cynthia, and the big fella on the end is Sterlo. Lily turned to look at Katie with a huge smile across her face. "You got to be careful of Fernando, he thinks he is king of the place, the cranky bugger, and will grab hold of your ponytail with his teeth and pull it when you turn your back to him" Katie laughed, hearing footsteps walking up behind them, she turned and jumped with a fright.

"I'm sorry, I didn't mean to scare you". The deep voice was the same one she heard on the phone. Katie smiled and shook it off. "I'm Gage, I see you have met my little sister Lily". He smiled as Lily wrapped her arms around him proudly. "Mum is looking for you". He said nodding his head at her she looked disappointed to not be included.

"I'll introduce you to my horse next time, Katie", Lily hugged her goodbye.

Gage stood 6ft 6inches tall, clean shaven, and wore the same brown, embroidered vest as Lily, a check-print, long sleeve, collared shirt, Wrangler Jeans and dogger boots. He had dirty blonde hair that sent loose curls from under his wide brimmed, black cowboy hat. His dimples were deep when he smiled. He seemed as gentle as he sounded on the phone. Katie fidgeted nervously.

"So, you have just moved to EagleHawk?". He put his hands in his vest pockets.

"Yeah, um, I wanted to start over somewhere new".

"Righto, well the job here is Monday to Friday, 7am starts, most days you will be done by 1 or 2pm"

He walked across to pick up the lead rope that had fallen on the floor in front of Clementine's stall, she hung her head over the half door, pushed her face into his shoulder, nestling into to him for a pat, sniffing eagerly.

"This is Clementine, she is a real sweetie". He fished into his pocket for a carrot. "She is mine and spoilt. Endeavour Park is run by my family, we have four casual staff who come in like you will if you choose to stay, it's a spelling stud, so horses that are injured, needing long term rest, or sometimes retiring is what we have here, most of them come and go after a few months, these guys in here, besides Clem, are from a riding school who's owner passed away, not sure how long they will be here yet".

"That's sad," Katie mumbled as she held her hand out to Barney to sniff. "I'm sorry I have not had any experience looking after horses, but I am a fast learner, I am willing to have a go".

Gage smiled and reached out to put his hand on her on the shoulder, she shifted her feet quickly taking a step back. Gage smiled awkwardly and put his hands back in his pockets.

"If you want to pop back out tomorrow at 7am for a trial day, that would be good, if you're happy with that?"

Katie smiled shyly, reaching out her hand. Gage looked at her hand visibly shaking, he took his hand out of his pocket and took hers, shaking it carefully. His hand was warm and his grip confident. Katie let go, smiled, and walked back down the breezeway over to Little Jim.

Katie came back a little before 7am the following morning. Lily met her at the breezeway doors with a big smile, clearly excited to see her. There were several other people around. Katie pushed the wheelbarrow along after Lily who appeared to love every minute of the responsibility she had been given to show Katie the morning jobs.

"Katie, this is my sister, Belinda".

Belinda Morgan grunted a hello to Katie, while talking on the phone and looked far from impressed to be interrupted to meet her. She was wearing the same uniform Lily wore and led an appaloosa mare into the wash bay. Lily walked Katie through the morning routine. Each of the horses in the indoor stalls were let out into their own adjoining outdoor run. Lily handed Katie a metal rake and showed her how to muck out the soiled saw dust. Katie caught on quickly scooping up the soiled areas with the rake and dumping it onto the wheelbarrow. Using another, plastic rake this time, the stall was raked so the saw dust spread across the floor evenly and slightly up the wall.

"How you going kiddo?" a voice called to Lily from the breezeway. Katie looked up to see an older couple standing, watching her. Lily introduced Katie.

"This is my Mum and Dad". Katie lent the rake against the wall of the stall and shook their hands.

"This is Dad, Roy, and Mum is me, Nancy, how are you finding it?" Roy didn't hang around long and soon vanished off into the tack room.

"Good, I am getting the hang of it, thank you for letting me come today" Katie was polite talking to them, not wanting to give a bad impression.

"Well, that's good to hear, I hope you will be back tomorrow then, there is tea and coffee in the staff room, help yourself if you need a break". Nancy left, walking in the same direction as Roy. Lily was stuck to Katie like glue, showing her the entire morning routine expertly from start to finish. Katie was thankful but also keen to have a quiet moment, making herself a cup of coffee in the staff room. Suddenly, someone opened the door, giving Katie such a fright, she dropped the cup, spilling the coffee on the floor.

"You must be the new girl, doing a great job already I see", The woman said walking into the staff room. She picked up her coat from the back of the chair, putting it on. "What are you staring at". she asked dryly as Gage walked in after her. Katie took the roll of paper towel from the bench. Gage looked down to see the broken pieces on the floor.

"I'm sorry, Ill replace the cup", she said wiping up the last of the spilt coffee. Gage stood up with pieces of the broken cup in his hand and reached for another cup from the hooks along the wall. Katie stood there silently.

"Damn right you will", Taylor accused.

"Enough, Taylor", Gage didn't even look at her, she huffed in disgust leaving the room, slamming the door behind her. "Please excuse my girlfriend, she can be rather direct at times, how do you have it?" He asked her softly.

"White with 2, lots of milk". Gage made her a coffee, stirring it quickly to build up a bit of froth. He put the spoon in the sink, passing her the cup. It was at that moment she noticed how big his hands were and little freckles he had on his thumb. She smiled and nodded in thanks, walking out nervously.

Nancy stood in the doorway at the other end. "She alright?" Gage made himself a coffee and leant against the bench in front of his Mum. "She is in a mood as usual", Gage mumbled to himself.

"I wasn't talking bout Taylor" Nancy's tone could have punched a hole in the wall.

"Mum I'm not doing this now".

At the end of her shift, Gage led Katie along the driveway out of the main stables to a back set of yards and a separate stable area between. The first yard had 5 donkeys that were being held for a rescue organization. Being around the donkeys made her soul smile. All 5 stood at the fence and let her pat them.

"They are so beautiful, being around them makes my heart happy".

Gage smiled watching her relax. He admired how genuinely she loved just standing there patting the donkeys, it was refreshing for a change to have that kind of peace around him.

"So, if you're happy to stay, we would love to give you the job, if you want to officially start on Monday I can drop a uniform into town over the weekend,"

"Thank you, you really don't understand how much this means to me". The smile on Katie's face was intoxicating, he couldn't help but smile back at her.

The separate stables to the side, were for the family horses, except Gage, he liked Clementine in with the others as she thrived on the company. The next 2 paddocks had mares that had been agisted there to foal, the next paddock, a little further along on its own, appeared empty. Gage stopped her there to turn around.

"What about that one?". She motioned to the furthest paddock, with the giant gum tree in the corner. Gage turned to look up at the tyre tracks through the grass to the isolated paddock in the corner.

"Only Dad tends to that one, the horse in there, she's dangerous."

Katie stood there watching the paddock fence for any movement, she felt a peculiar energy come over her, something she had never felt before, goosebumps prickled up her back, there was something about that paddock that took hold of her without even seeing what was in there.

"Why is she dangerous?"

Gage walked a few paces past her to look towards the paddock as the mare walked into view.

"My Grandfather bought that horse, she had been abused, he was the only one who could get close to her", Gage put his hands in his pockets and started walking past her back to the stables.

Katie was horrified that the horse had been left there. How could someone just buy an abused horse and dump it there.

"What kind of person would just leave her in there on her own, where is your grandfather now?". She yelled after him.

Gage stopped still in a moment of shock, then kept walking back to the stables. He didn't look back at her when he answered.

"He's dead".

Chapter 5

Katie sat in the portable gazebo at the blowhole with Dot, eating strawberries, looking through a booklet of local rental listings. Dot and she had become good friends ever since day one, sharing a coffee most afternoons to talk about their days. Dot was a widow and enjoyed Katie's company.

"How is the car going?" Dot asked her keenly.

Katie bought Little Jim from Louise for $500. She absolutely loved her 1989 bomb.

"Dot, I'm not sure you have given me the right list". Katie seemed confused.

 The strange part about these listings was the names all had the word 'DOO' in the title. Doolittle, Doodah, Doo-drop-In, Make-Doo. It was a small beach village called Dootown, there were 40 houses in this area with doo in their name. It was well known, and the tourists loved it. There were a few Doo-shacks available for rent.

Dot laughed quietly as Katie read through the names.

 She applied for number 145 Dootown Rd.; a shack called 'I don't give a doo dah".

"I'll feel like an idiot saying I live at 'I don't give a doo dah" Katie laughed so hard the coffee came out her nose. Dot passed her a tissue.

"It's good to see you happy". Dot felt like an adopted mother to her. The kind, caring, and loyal kind that she always wished for. Katie had even felt comfortable enough to confide in her how hard her life had been and how she escaped from Rick and her childhood. It was good to get it off her chest, it was a weight lifted that's for sure.

That afternoon Katie and Dot pulled into 145 Dootown rd. It was a small, 2-bedroom shack surrounded by bush. It had a simple looking outside, timber cladding on the walls and a small porch. There was a carport at the end of the driveway. The real estate agent showed her through. The agent, Amy, was Dot's niece which was helpful. The inside was small, the timber cladding repeated itself inside also. It had a small, galley-style kitchen and was partly furnished, which was what attracted her, as she literally still had one duffle bag to her name. She listed Dot as her emergency contact and Amy agreed to give her a 6 month lease with no bond as a favour to her Aunt and was respectful of the request to put the lease in Dot's name not hers, just in case. The agent handed her the keys and the lease agreement.

"There is one issue I need to address", the agent said, "There is a cat that lives here, it's been here for years, unfortunately, he comes with the house, his name is Fin".

Katie's eyes lit up, a cat, she liked cats.

"Thanks lovey, you'll be over for dinner on Saturday night won't you", Dot reminded her niece as she walked her out to her car.

A few days later, after saying goodbye to the Lufra apartment, Katie stood at the front door looking at her new home. Her own home. She fought back tears. She had come a long way in the last month. The day she took that first step off the bus, she never imagined that she would be standing there in this moment. Everything had come together. She had a job and a new home. Katie was in no way frail. She had grown emotionally solid over years of being in foster homes and finding herself in such a toxic relationship. She was guarded of her feelings, she had never really felt truly loved by anyone, she wasn't even sure if Rick ever loved her, she was more a play toy for him, she had never been in love before. She had soul searched since stowing away in the back of the semi-trailer. She was learning to love herself more.

Dot had given her several garbage bags full of blankets, sheets, and pillowcases. Katie heard her phone beep a text notification. It was Gage, asking where he could drop off her uniform. She still felt terrible about how the conversation ended the last time she saw him. She texted back her address. How amazing it felt to simply tell someone where she lived knowing she was ok, even if her home was called 'I don't give a doo dah".

Gage pulled into her driveway in a white Prado, it had the Endeavour Park logo on the side. He got out carrying a box up to her porch, putting it down on the top step, as she opened the door.

"Hey". She smiled shyly.

"Mum sent in a heap of uniforms, hopefully the sizes are ok, you will need to buy a pair of boots, oh and there is an employment form on top, if you can fill it out and bring it back when you start." Gage nodded and started to walk away.

"Gage, I'm sorry, I was out of line the other day,". Gage turned to look at her. She could see the pain in his face at the thought of her wanting to talk. "Maybe one day you could tell me more about it".

Gage sighed, "One day".

Katie drove Little Jim into Port Arthur to do some shopping. She found the plaza and parked under the cover. Walking around Kmart, she filled a trolley with household items quickly. She had everything from knives and forks to a toaster, a dinner set, fry pan, the works. Unloading the trolley of bags into Little Jim, the realization of how small he was was setting in. She decided to drive back to Eaglehawk Neck, unload and then go back to the next store.

The day dragged on, by 4pm she arrived home with the last load. 'I don't give a doo dah' came with a fridge, it was old, but it worked. The groceries fitted neatly in the pantry cupboard. Katie took a bottle of wine from the fridge, when she heard a little meow from the front door. The excitement of having a cat she couldn't contain. Carefully she opened the door, and an orange fluff ball marched in, full of attitude and self-importance, meowing his complaints loudly, walking through the lounge into the kitchen and sat beside the fridge.

"Oh, hello, you must be Fin,"

He let out a long, drawn-out, strangled noise.

"Righto then, I see, so you're hungry". She smiled and opened the pantry door.

"Isn't it your lucky day", she took out a can of cat food that she bought from the supermarket. "Are sardines ok, sir?"

He let out another long-winded meow. She opened the can, scraping out a few spoons into a plastic cat bowl, another thing she bought when in town in anticipation of this moment.

As Fin ate noisily, Katie wanted to celebrate life, happiness, and her new pet, she had never had a pet before. The fact she had a pantry full of food was something to celebrate or even a pantry at all, not having to ask permission to eat something or being told she could only have showers not baths. She opened the bottle of Pink Moscato and poured herself a coffee cup full.

"Knew there was something I forgot to buy, wine glasses" she said to Fin. She walked into the bathroom, placing the cup on the side of the old clawfoot bath. It was white on the inside and a dark grey painted outside that was flaking off in parts. It stood quite far into the middle of the room. She ran the water, throwing in a bath bomb that made the water purple. She lit 3 tea light candles and put them on the end of the bath. Sinking into the water, the steam rose in mystical swirls as she sipped her wine. In her life, since she was a young child, she had reinvented herself over and over, after every foster home, after every setback, and now she had done so again after Rick. Katie had had so much loss in her life, loss of family, her childhood, she didn't even know where her father was, he left before she was born, her mother was a drug addict which was why she ended up in foster care. The last time she heard about her she was in jail. The one thing Katie longed for was the feeling of family, and to feel love. It's funny how easily the abuse from Rick washed away as she lay in the bath. She was determined to live life to the fullest now, she felt like she had this amazing chance to make something meaningful of her life. Now she just had to find what it was that made her heartbeat that little bit faster, the things that inspired her.

Fin invited himself into the bathroom not long after feasting, taking up residence on the stool beside the sink. She watched him cleaning himself. He was a dark ginger, had white under his chin and on one of his paws, his fur was long like a Persian but not a smooth and well-kept house cat, rather dishevelled, patchy, and dull. He had a few small patches of fur missing off his head and half an ear, obviously been into fights. He crouched down making himself at home. His purring was one of the most comforting sounds she had ever heard.

Chapter 6

Katie arrived early; the fog was thick. She had been working at Endeavour Park for 3 weeks now and loved every part of the job and walked with a new-found, proud confidence. She parked Little Jim beside a fancy looking White Mercedes. As she arrived for work, Taylor stood in the breezeway door looking unimpressed. Katie wasn't scared of the stuck-up horse princess, Gage's partner obviously thought very highly of herself.

"Please don't park *that* beside my car, it doesn't give a great impression", Taylor snickered. Katie wasn't going to be bullied by her. No way! She had been through enough ridicule in her life and with that newfound confidence she smiled happily at her as she walked past.

"Have you not had your coffee yet this morning? Best get on to that, won't you".

Taylor stood shocked, mouth open and blood boiling. Katie imagined licking her finger and putting an invisible notch on her wall of conquest. Nothing was going to dampen her shine today, she felt happy, just loving life. Taylor's only job was to exercise the horses, she was a national medallist in dressage and jumping on her horse named Enchanting Symphony who was stabled separately from the agisted horses. She was expected to make the Olympic team at the upcoming trials. Taylor felt her mare was far too important to be housed next to what she called 'riding school nags'.

Katie started on the indoor stables as usual. Barney was first. He was quite a funny fellow. He liked to rest his muzzle on her shoulder, wiggle his lips around and touch his tongue to your skin, the long hairs on his chin tickling your cheek as he did it. Each stable had a sliding handle that opened the door in the back of the stable which let the horses out into an adjoining outside yard.

"Are you right there?" Katie took off his blanket and opened the stall door to let him out into his outdoor pen. She moved onto the big grey, Leeroy. Taking his blankets off, giving him some ear scratches before letting him out. Marilyn was white and the graceful queen of the stables, holding her head high. Sherlock was black with a white blaze down his face, he was older than all the others, kind of the grandfather of the bunch, the one the riding school would have people ride who had never been before and a bit scared. A big gentle rocking horse. Across to the other side she opened Fernando's door, keeping her back to the wall, taking off his blanket and letting him out, she wasn't going to get bitten today. Dodge, a part Clydesdale, was the biggest. She stood on a blue milk crate to get herself high enough to pull his rug off. Big and slow. He took his time walking out into the day yard. Angel and Cynthia, two Arabians had serious attitude problems. She didn't waste any time getting out of their way. Finally, there was Sterlo, he was her favourite. He just stood there, lazy and fat. He was on a diet which clearly wasn't working. He loved to eat and would sniff you all over, looking for treats. His beautiful dark eyes were deep and soulful.

Katie hung Sterlo's blanket on the rail outside his stable and came back across to Clementine. She always left her till the end. She was Gage's horse and just like she did to him, she rubbed her face into her shoulder sniffing at her pockets for carrots. She was a soft grey over her body which turned darker down her legs. She hung her blanket on the rail letting her out into the fresh foggy air.

Taylor watched her mucking out the stables, filling the wheelbarrow with soiled saw dust.

"You certainly have a knack for shovelling shit". Her high pitch, posh voice matched her to a tee. Nose high in the air, giggling to herself with a pompous self-importance.

Lily listened to Taylor give Katie a hard time. Katie finished the last of the stables and pushed the wheelbarrow forward leaving it outside the staffroom door, stopping to make a coffee.

"Good morning, Lily, how are you today". She greeted. Taylor sat at the centre table eating her toast.

"Amazing, I have a riding lesson today, I can't wait". Lily was bouncing off the walls with excitement as she wiped up her plate. Taylor just rolled her eyes at the teenage antics; she had no patience at all.

"I've never ridden a horse myself so I can only imagine how exciting it must be", Katie put her arm around Lily with an affectionate hug and made her coffee. Taylor huffed and smirked at the fact that Katie had never ridden before. She stood up and put her plate in the sink, not caring about cleaning her own dishes.

"Stick to what you do best, stable girl". Taylor said to Katie as she walked out of the staff room door. Katie shrugged her shoulders at Lily, suddenly hearing a scream followed by a bout of swearing. Katie and Lily came out of the staff room door to see Nancy and Belinda doing their best to hold in their laughter at an upturned wheelbarrow and Taylor sitting amongst the soiled bedding.

"What idiot left that there, I fell right into it". Katie smiled and picked up the wheelbarrow.

"I see you have landed yourself in a bit of shit there," Katie extended her hand to Taylor who stared at her with contempt, refusing to let Katie give her a hand up. Taylor walked furiously down the breezeway towards the back set of private stables to shower.

Katie carried a bucket of grain in each hand for the donkeys. They greeted her in an orchestra of honking. She poured the feed in two separate feed containers trying to encourage them to take their time eating it instead of hoovering it down like 4-legged, furry vacuum cleaners.

They were just the most beautiful creatures. Their big eyes and fluffy ears made her happy, from her head to her toes, the warm feeling they gave her was special. That unexpected flutter of goosebumps up her arms instantly sent a coldness down her spine as she looked towards the end of the dirt road where the ute tracks in the long grass started. That paddock was calling her, she could feel the energy pulling at her. Katie walked to the end of the dirt to stand at the edge of the grass, looking over at the isolated paddock. She could see the horse looking directly at her. A unique, cool blonde face peering through the timber rails. She was too far away to make out the horse's features. Katie looked around. There was no one, no movement back at the stables. A nervous pain in the depths of her stomach nearly grounded her to the spot. She walked slowly along one of the tyre tracks in the grass. The grass was tall, up to her waist in some parts which soon had her disappearing down the slight incline out of sight from the stables. A shield of nature hiding her from any people watching, just like the rain did the night she left Rick. It was at least twenty meters of track before she came to the wooden railings of the paddock edge. The paddock was so big it disappeared into the distance past the gum tree, downhill to a collection of smaller trees which looked to be a creek. One foot at a time she stood on the bottom rail, so she was tall enough to rest her elbows over the top rail. There was no sign of the horse that she had seen before. Katie made a kissing noise with her lips then stood silently listening for any movement. She wasn't about to give up so easily, she was drawn to this paddock and couldn't explain why. Katie got down from the railing and sat in the grass alongside the fence, humming a lullaby one of her foster mums had sung to her when she was 7, picking grass, breaking it up and making a little pile, when she heard the grass in front of her rustling. Katie kept humming, not looking up, making out to just ignore the careful hoof steps that came towards her, stopping a few meters from the rails. Katie kept humming, shifting herself very slowly trying to catch a glimpse without scaring her off. Katie could see a patterned, blonde body and deep brown legs through the grass, she carefully moved onto her hands and knees. Still humming softly, she reached into her vest pocket to grasp her fingers around a chunk of carrot she had kept for Clementine. She crept forward and pushed her hand under the bottom rail, leaving the carrot inside the paddock and sat back where she was before, keeping her head down.

The sniffing and snorting noise through the grass sounded eager but guarded. The horse took a few steps forward to stand directly in front of her. Katie was scared, her stomach burned like fire as the horse sniffed along the grass, working her way over to the carrot, wiggling her lips a bit to pick it up. Katie lifted her head up shyly to see a sad looking face peering through the bottom set of rails, looking directly at her, eating the carrot. The mare was buckskin, a unique, dapple blonde all over, with patterns of darker and lighter flickering through her coat and darker mane and tail. A tear fell onto Katies cheek as she looked at her beautifully broken face. She had a thick, hairless scar that ran the entire length on one side of her face, she was blind in one eye. Gage said the trainer used to abuse her, bash her, the injury to her face must have been initially horrific to leave her with such a brutal looking scar.

"Hello girl", Katie spoke softly. "I'm Abby, but people call me Katie now". The big mare just stood there, her head low to the ground, watching her with her good eye and just listening. "I don't know what you have been through, but I am a little bit broken too".

The mare made a little nicker noise. Katie reached her hand out. To rest it on the bottom railing. The horse seemed curious but scared and suddenly bolted off down the paddock.

Katie walked back down the track onto the dirt and past the donkeys. Gage stood in the breezeway sharing his sandwich with Clementine.

"Where have you been?". he asked curiously. Katie was instantly guilt ridden and she always found it hard to make up stories on the spot. She felt a wave of sudden anxiety wash over her as he questioned her. Controlling her breathing and calming down she gathered her thoughts.

"I was talking to the donkeys..ah..before I went home" she stumbled on her words, brushing the grass from the front of her vest.

"I heard you had a run in with Taylor this morning".

Katie didn't know what to say. Was she in trouble here or was he going to have a laugh about it, the angst would have been written all over her face. "I'm not angry at you, just try and stay out of her way yeah, she can be pretty full on".

Katie nodded as he turned to walk away.

"Gage?". Katie nervously blurted out. He turned on one heel to face her. "I need you to tell me about the horse, in the paddock with the big tree".

Gage glanced down the breeze way and then back at her, the shard of grass stuck in her hair made sense to him and he, very quickly, realised where she had been. Gage sighed. He didn't want to talk about it, it was as plain as day, but he knew deep down she wasn't going to let up until he told her, he sighed loudly, turning to face her.

"Her racing name is 'For the Love of January', most knew of her when she raced because she was a buckskin. It's not common to see racehorses in that colour. Walter, my Pop, used to just call her simply Jan, she won quite a few group one races, was even looking like she was going to make it into The Melbourne Cup, Pop had watched her run a few times, said she was a gold mine because she was always so hot headed once under saddle, tended to jump out of the gates like she had a score to settle every time". Gage walked closer to Katie, his hands in his pockets.

"She took a fall on her last group one and killed the jockey, the trainer had her tied in the mounting yard after the race and took to her with a star picket, everyone just stood there and watched because they were too scared to intervene. Not Pop though, on the spot he ran in and beat the fuck out of him, bought the horse back home and fixed her up, ended up with a few months jail for the flogging he gave the bloke, but the beating traumatized her, and she started lashing out at everyone who tried to go near her, except Pop".

Katie stood completely still, her mouth open, numb to the core as she listened, she put her hand to her mouth in thought.

"Before he died, Pop had this big dream of teaching Jan to jump. He started her not long before he got sick, he wanted to enter her into the Hobart Novice Opens comp, she is an ex-racer of all things, but he had her jumping and she was good at it, he was even going to ride her in the comp too, I had no idea he could ride like that. As pop was dying, Dad promised him he wouldn't get rid of her", Gage shrugged and started to walk away, turning to look back.

"She will stay there for the rest of her life as promised".

Chapter 7.

Katie lay on the couch in her loungeroom. Dot washed up her coffee cup after dinner and sat beside her. Katie told her about Jan, and the other events of the week at Endeavour Park.

"Taylor is a gold digger, has been her whole life, the only reason she is hanging onto Gage is the fact his family owns that stud, and they are her major sponsors for the Olympic trials", Dot's cold tone could have cracked glass. "I have never liked that girl, but I am glad Gage told you about the horse".

"I feel a connection to her, I can't explain why, Dot", Katie smiled watching Fin loudly announce his presence to the universe, walking in, licking his chops after his dinner and sitting with a hard stare until Katie lifted the blanket letting him wedge himself against her back under it.

"Old Walter Morgan knew horses better than anyone, if he reckoned, she could jump I'd bet she can". Dot picked up her handbag.

"Well, I better be off home love,". Dot kissed her on the cheek and left. "I am looking forward to the next episode of the story about this horse".

Katies phone beeped, she picked it up to check the notification. It was Ross River Vets.

"New cat has arrived; think he has stopped looking for the old one". Katie was happy to read it but also gutted inside that some other poor girl may be about to go through all the things she had. It also gave her a sense of relief, she had been gone 3 months, it was an amazing feeling that he wasn't looking for her anymore.

Before going to bed, Katie searched the internet for Jan. It wasn't long before she found article upon article on 'For The Love of January'. It seemed Jan was more famous than Gage made it seem. According to the Hobart Racing page archives, Jan's winnings before the accident were over a million dollars. The trainer was known for his stern approach to training his horses but the incident with Jan shed light on just how bad it was. Tom Dolandson, of Dolandson racing was charged with multiple counts of animal cruelty for his treatment of 4 horses in his care, one in particular, Jan. The article went on to talk about her being retired from racing after a debilitating scene that ended in Mr Dolandson being hospitalized after Mr Walter Morgan assaulted him. Both men later facing jail time over the altercation. There were hundreds of photos of Jan when racing. She was and still is a unique looking horse.

Katie arrived early, parking Little Jim on the far end of the carpark, next to an old red horse float to try and keep the peace with Taylor. The day was miserable, misty rain and heavy fog hung low above the grass. Taylor worked each of the indoor stabled horses one by one in the indoor arena before her own. Katie hung her head around the corner to watch her on Marilyn, easily going over the jumps that were set up on one side. The indoor arena was huge, it had a sandy floor with high vaulted ceilings. The far end of the arena was open to let the air circulate with two enormous sliding metal doors.

Belinda rode Sherlock, he was indeed lazy, he wasn't having a bar of jumps or fancy trotting, he simply walked around the edge, doing exactly as he pleased. Lily also was riding close to where Katie was hiding. Gage stood in the middle as Lily rode Gypsy, her palomino pony in a 20m circle, Gage was giving instructions to her as she went around. He was gentle with his little sister, very attentive but also firm in his instruction. Lily saw her and waved; Gage turned to see her watching.

"That's enough for today, Lil, walk him a few laps around the arena to cool down and take him back to his stable and brush him out".

Katie stepped back and started walking back to the indoor stable.

"Not so fast".

Katie stopped still, pivoting on one heel to face him.

"Why don't you go and get Sterlo, it's your turn". Gage pointed to the saddle sitting over the rail in front of her. Katie felt the colour drain from her face, he walked over to lean his elbows across the saddle, looking right at her with a cheeky smile. Katie didn't argue, in fact she couldn't get away fast enough. Opening Sterlo's door, she clipped the lead rope to his halter and walked him down the breezeway, he gave off an excited, fat prance the closer they got to the arena. Gage took his lead rope and secured him to the bailing twine that was tied to the arena wall. Gage ushered her over.

"Grab that bridle there", he pointed. "Now, lucky for you, Sterlo will stand here and let you do whatever you want, any other time we do it this way". Gage undid the nose band of the halter and slid it down his neck, still keeping him secure while also allowing the bridal to easily go on, He held the bridle with the brow band looped around his thumb and ran his fingers up Sterlo's face, holding the bit flat in his hand at his mouth, encouraging him to take the bit. He played with the cold metal in his mouth, moving his tongue around it. Gage secured the reins to the twine and undid the halter, hanging it on a hook on the arena wall "ok, Saddle pad next". Katie passed him the pad. "No, you can do it". She placed it on his back. Gage holding his fingers on his withers to guide her how far to pull it up. Gage lifted the stirrup over the seat and picked it up, showing her how to correctly hold it with one hand slightly under each end. He placed the saddle on, adjusting it at the wither again.

"Now, reassure him, pat him, and reach through to get the girth".

She did exactly what he said, she looped the buckle through and fastened it on the last notch. "Ok, so because Sterlo is a bit round, it's going to be a tight fit, walk him over to that wall and back". Katie untied his reins and walked him across, the leather saddle creaking as he walked. She couldn't help but laugh at the small grunts he let out as he walked. Gage tightened the girth a bit more with another groan.

Gage passed her a helmet. "Up you get". Gage was serious, she was terrified, but put her foot up into the stirrup iron and heaved herself up. "This is going to be your new job, to ride Sterlo in here every day, he needs the exercise, and he will be good for you to learn on."

"I don't know how to ride". She was scared, looking down at him, he took hold of her hand and passed her the reins.

"I am going to teach you, chunky boy here isn't fit enough to give you too much trouble, perfect to learn on, take the reins, both hands, elbows in, relax, give him a little squeeze, and ask him to walk on". He showed her how to correctly hold the reins in her fingers.

Katie gently squeezed her knees, and he reluctantly moved forward. Gage let him walk out to the end of the lunge rein, and ushered Katie to keep him out, encouraging him to move forward and not stop. She walked easily. He instructed her randomly various things like back straight, relax your arms, elbows in. It was the same instructions over and over reminding her. She was getting the hang of it quickly. Taylor watched from the other end; you could feel the green-eyed monster in the air.

"Ok, now we will take him into a trot, let him know again, like you did before, and you're just going to sit one beat, rise one beat."

Katie looked across at Gage, his eyes reassuring her she squeezed her knees again. Sterlo happily moved forward.

"You're doing well, good job".

Katie felt a wave of accomplishment wash over her. She trotted easily for 10 minutes.

"Do you want to try a canter?"

 Katie nodded.

"Again, like before you're going to ask him to move forward into a canter, you are going to sit into this gait, relax, and move with him".

Katie did what Gage said. Sterlo leapt forward into a slow canter, snorting and complaining with every step but eager to do it. She sat beautifully; it was like being on a big fat rocking horse.

"Go girl". He encouraged her.

Taylor, her green eyes embedding deep into Katie's flesh, wasn't having a bar of Gage giving her attention. She jumped Marilyn over the last jump and turned her sharply up the middle of the arena, letting her go at a hard run, startling Sterlo. He stopped suddenly on the spot, sending an unprepared Katie over his head into the sand. Taylor laughed, pulling Marilyn up at the open doors at the far end, she walked her out of the arena, nose in the air nearly as high as Marilyn's.

Belinda pulled Sherlock up beside Sterlo, quickly sliding down to help her.

Gage talked calmly to Sterlo that it was ok, passing the reins to Belinda, he ran down the arena after Taylor. Sterlo stood there with no care in the world. Katie was in tears. She had skin off her elbow as it took the brunt of the fall. Nothing was broken, it was more the shock of falling that had rattled her.

"You're ok, I've had so many falls over the years, I guarantee this will be the first of many", Belinda rubbed Katie's back and led both horses to the wall, securing the reins again back at the bailing twine. Katie brushed herself off.

"I'm ok," She took off the helmet. "What's her problem?" Katie asked as she unbuckled Sterlo's girth, pulling the saddle and pad off to hang them on the rail where they were before.

"She feels threatened by you I'd say, she always has been a really jealous person and Gage was giving his time and attention to you, she doesn't like it". Belinda pulled Sherlock's saddle off, hanging it where Katie did, sliding both bridles off and putting their halters back on.

"Why does he stay with her?"

Belinda shrugged her shoulders. "They have been on and off again for years, broken up a few times and back together, one day someone else will come along that will change that I hope," Belinda looked at her with a cheeky smile.

"Hopefully sooner rather than later, are you ok to lead him back? I can come back for him if you can't."

"No, I can, I'm ok". Katie led Sterlo back down the arena and into the breezeway to his stall. She gave him a quick brush down and slid his rug over his back with a slight grunt, holding her elbow.

"Let me help you," the deep voice came from behind her. Gage opened the stall door, and she stood aside while he buckled his rug on. He rubbed the big fella on the neck, "Good boy".

Katie patted him, pulling a piece of carrot from her vest pocket. "He did good when I fell off, he didn't seem too worried".

Gage took her arm in his hand, she instinctively edged away at first as he touched her, he looked closely at her, worried, looking at her elbow and sighed. "That's years of being in a riding school, they learn to stay calm, he is a good boy, come on", Gage opened the stall door and led her by the hand into the staff room. Reaching on top of the fridge for the first aid kit, he squeezed some clear, saline solution on a cotton pad and gently wiped the blood and sand away from the graze. She jolted a few times as he touched her.

"Why do you do that, are you scared of me?"

Katie took the cotton ball from his hand. She wanted to run away from him, but a part of her wanted to let him help her.

"This will be ok now". She backed away from him and left quickly avoiding the situation completely.

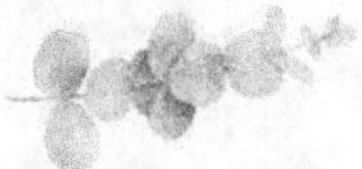

Katie lay in the hot, steaming bath listening to the rain on the tin roof. Fin sat on guard, as he always did, on the stool near the sink. Her elbow was sore, the bruising was starting to come out already. She had been injured far worse than this before but somehow this seemed to hurt so much more. A notification bell went off on her phone, she looked at it resting on the side of the clawfoot tub. Sitting up, she dried her hands off and opened the text from Gage.

'I hope you are ok; I am sorry for what happened today'. She re-read the words a few times before another one came through. 'I am sorry if I scare you'. Katie found it hard to read it. She wasn't scared of him, she felt safer in his presence than anyone else, something she never thought she would feel, her reactions sometimes come on their own, a reflex to not trusting people.

'I am not scared of you' she wrote back. He wrote back to her instantly.

'Maybe you can tell me about it one day'.

Katie smiled and replied, "One day".

Chapter 8.

Katie sat in the grass on the inside of Jan's paddock. Humming the same lullaby as she did every time she came. Every day Jan has become more and more interested in getting closer to her. Today she thought she would go a bit further. She had her pockets loaded with carrots to encourage her. Jan stood a few meters away from her, apprehensive at first. The key seemed to be to not look at her and keep her head down. She took a bite from one of the carrots, deliberately crunching noisily with her mouth open. Jan's ears pricked up and she took a few more steps towards her. Her colour was unlike anything she has seen, a dapple, dark and light buck skin coat and dark tail. Extremely unusual for a thoroughbred.

"Oh, do you want some?" Katie asked the big blonde horse softly, taking another bite again crunching loudly.

Half an hour later, Jan was close enough that she could have touched her. She slowly held her hand out flat resting it on her knee, 3 chunks of carrot sitting on it. Jan tossed her head up and down, she wanted it, but she was hesitant to take it out of her hand. With her other hand Katie took another bite, loudly crunching.

Tossing her head up again, Jan slowly hung her head low, right in front of Katie's hands. Jan's nostrils flaring as she smelt the carrots. Wiggling her hairy bottom lip she touched Katie's hand, the hairs tickling her palm. She took the first piece, then the second and the third. Tossing her head up nickering she lowered her head again resting her muzzle in the palm of Katie's hand. She smiled happily, sat still for a moment and then moved her fingers to scratch her chin. Katie couldn't hide her excitement; she was finally earning her trust. Jan's face was so much worse up close.

"I'll be coming back tomorrow, do you like apples? I might bring you one". Katie moved her hand to scratch further under her chin, as soon as she tried to touch her face she backed away.

Katie walked back to the stables. The dirt track was full of mud puddles since the early morning rain, and she couldn't help but childishly step in them on the way back.

Roy Morgan waited in the breeze way for Katie. She nervously approached him.

"How is Jan today?"

Katie looked guilty; she had been sneaking up to see her every day. She thought no one had noticed her going there but obviously Roy had.

"How close have you managed to get to her?". Roy looked at her seriously. He wasn't joking around.

Katie told him about her progress from day one till now. Roy looked flabbergasted. He scratched his head in amusement.

"I have been trying to get near her for nearly 2 years and you're telling me today, she ate from your hand". Katie nodded proudly. "No one other than my father, Walter, could get close enough to touch her"

"I guess I just understand her, not sure why, but I have been drawn to her from the moment I got here".

Roy paced up and down the breezeway while Katie contemplated if she was about to get fired.

"Don't mention this to Gage, keep it between us for now". Roy seriously looked at Katie.

"So, you're ok with me seeing her again tomorrow?"

Roy smiled, nodded his approvement, walking away deep in thought, he turned back to her.

"Oh, by the way, Sherlock has been adopted, he will be picked up tomorrow afternoon, can you make sure all of his tack is in front of the stall as the new owner will take it also".

The grunting coming from the last stable was getting louder by the minute. Katie nodded.

"Ok, ok, Sterlo, I'm coming". Katie led the excited chunky fellow out for a ride.

The next day Katie walked down to see Jan. Pockets bulging with treats. After talking to Roy, she felt so much more energized and determined to make friends with Jan. Walking down the tyre track this time she started calling her name before she got there. The nickering started quickly. Jan rushed from under the big gum tree right up to the gate. This was the first time Katie had called her before coming into the paddock, the first time she physically stood next to her properly. She was tall. Her all-over blonde coat was smooth and shiny. She had more than just the scars on her face though, they were scattered across the whole of her body. Katie dug in her pockets with a carrot in both hands. Jan stood there, sniffing towards her. She always stood with her good eye facing her. She held out her hand and she took the carrot instantly. Katie had worked hard to build up a bond with Jan, even if it was bribing her with carrots.

Today, Katie finally had a breakthrough. She reached out and touched her on the shoulder and down onto her belly scratching hard with her nails just behind her front leg. Jan stretched out her neck and started dribbling.

"Oh, I see, is that the right spot?" Jan sighed and made a deep groaning noise.

"I have something else for you", Katie reached into her back pocket and pulled out a shiny red apple. Jan instantly seemed interested.

"Hang on, you have to earn it". Katie took a big bite, noisily eating the piece in her mouth, the fresh apple smell had Jan sniffing the air, nickering happily. She held the rest of it in one hand down at her side. Jan lowered her head, her blind side fully facing Katie for the first time. Jan seemed relaxed still. This was a new level of vulnerability for Jan, this was the closest to her bad side that she had ever been. Katie let her get closer to the apple, her lips trying to get it, but she pulled back. Katie started to hum the same lullaby she had done before. Jan relaxed even more; her shoulder twitched as she let the tension go. Katie touched her neck, she pat her gently, humming softly. She ran her hand along Jan's jaw, to her cheek, gently patting it, she

could see Jan letting go to her, she ran her hand along
her cheek to touch the bottom of the scar, just above her
nostril. The roaring nervous pain that ran through
Katie's veins was like a hurricane, but she pushed it
aside and kept going. Katie ran her hand up Jan's nose,
following the scar towards her ear. Jan pushed her
head into Katies chest for the first time, her battered
face resting in her hands. She gently ran her fingers
from the front of her ears to the nostril, the full length
of the scar. Katie began to cry, softly the tears fell onto
her cheek as Jan sensed it. The significance of what
was happening was immense. She held the rest of the
apple in her hand for Jan. She crunched loudly as she
took it in her mouth.

Katie was woken suddenly after dozing off on the
couch, a car door, she half woke up but still dozed. She
heard another car door close which fully woke her up.
She peaked through the front curtains to see a red car
driving away. Katie opened the front door. There was
a parcel on the front step. She looked around, there
was no movement in the surrounding bushland, no
movement up the driveway. The yard was silent
except for a few magpies walking around the front
grass. Bending down she picked up the box and took it
back inside.

The postmark was an instant red flag for her.
Cannondale, Western Australia. She checked her
phone. There were no new messages from Ross River
vets. Katie sat at the little round dining table staring at
the box. The ball of knots in her stomach was heavy,

tornados of what if's churned through her body. Was it a bomb? Or some other threat, should she call someone to come and sit with her to open it? Should she call the police? The box sat on her table for nearly 2 hours while she procrastinated. There was no return address. She finally got a knife from the drawer in the kitchen and slid it under the flap, where the sticky tape started, and ran the blade along the seam. She opened the lid carefully. Whatever it was, it was wrapped up in white tissue paper. There was an envelope on top. Katie opened the envelope carefully. She slid out the folded, foolscap, lined paper realizing it was from Rosanna. She was going back to the Dominican Republic as she no longer had a job.

Katie nearly choked reading the words. Rick was dead. Katie opened the tissue paper to see a newspaper with an article on the front page, titled. 'Four people dead after truck stop blaze'

Katie read the article. Police have confirmed four fatalities. Rick Linnell, truck stop owner, Sally Gleeson, Emma Greybornn, and Cliff Hammond all confirmed dead. Cliff was a regular truckie who she saw at least once a week when she was there, he was always kind to her. She read on.

'Owner Rick Linnell and his partner were caught inside the truck stop as the fire took hold quickly. The cause of the fire was believed to be a tragic accident, a car driven by local high school teacher, Miss Emma Greybornn, ignited shortly after hitting the fuel pump, the initial explosion was heard up to 5kms away. It took local fire fighters 3 hours to extinguish the blaze and they remained on scene till the morning, removing hazardous fuel remaining in danger of reignition.

Katie read the same sentence several times. Rick's partner, his victim maybe after her, she would never know for sure though, her name was Sally. Her picture was in the article. She looked young, had blonde hair and the article suggested she was from Sydney. Maybe he could have loved her, he might not have done what he did to her to this girl. She felt sorry for her. Part of her felt an insatiable relief at the thought of him being dead, he literally would never look for her now. There was now nothing to hide from but also sad for the others who lost their lives.

Also in the package was a small intricate metal, engraved box. Inside the box was a necklace. It was a blue stone, with white ocean-like wave patterns, surrounded by a solid silver border. She instantly remembered it as being the same necklace Rosanna wore daily. It was called Larimar. Rosanna would say it was a worry stone. Used by her family for generations to help bring peace and serenity to the home. When worn it was believed it would bring peace and calming energy, ward away negativity. This was Rosanna's way of saying goodbye and good luck. She couldn't have left without her help. The letter read that all she hoped for was that she would be happy. Indeed, she was.

Chapter 9.

Lily sat on top of a hay bale, polishing her saddle. The tension in the air was so thick, you could almost reach out and touch it. Taylor was in a foul mood, nothing unusual for her, she walked back and forth from her stable loading saddles, blankets, and various shaped bags into her float. Katie looked confused, she had never seen Taylor look like this, hair a mess and wearing baggy tracksuit pants and ugg boots which was completely out of character for the horse princess. If looks could kill it was obvious she would have been dead on day one of meeting her, if not over and over again every day since.

Katie let Sterlo back into his stall after his morning ride. "Are you ok Lily?", Katie asked her carefully.

"Yeah, guess so."

Katie wasn't sure exactly what was going on, looking around at the chaos unfolding, Nancy had stacked boxes beside Taylor's white Mercedes, the tack room had been rummaged through and a pile of brushes and lead ropes were stacked high in the breeze way.

"Mum and Taylor had a big argument last night".

Katie sat down slowly on the feed bin across from her.

"Did you want to talk about it?". Katie asked her.

Lily shrugged her shoulders keeping her head down as Taylor stomped past with another bag, dragging it behind her, she pegged a brush into the pile as she walked past.

"Gage and Taylor have broken up, again".

Katie covered her mouth with her hand to try and shield her gaping shock from being obvious when Taylor stormed past them again. Katie thought back on the last few months she had been at Endeavour Park, she couldn't recall a time she ever saw them even touch each other, Taylor was always bitchy, nose right up in the clouds looking down on everyone.

"It's probably a good thing because they fight all the time". Lily sighed.

Katie rubbed Lily's shoulder in comfort. Taylor came back towards them.

"Do you need any help?". Katie asked, hoping not to find herself on the receiving end of a brush hurtling through the air.

Taylor stopped in front of Katie. Even though Taylor had been nothing but unwelcoming and mean to her she genuinely felt sorry for her.

"Why would I want your unpolished, grubby hands touching my stuff?"

Katie didn't say anything, just raised an eyebrow. Nancy dropped an empty box beside the pile of tack in the breezeway.

"Hurry up and get off my property". Nancy was direct but polite.

Taylor pushed a clump of hair that had fallen from her messy bun beside her ear and swallowed hard as she dragged the bag to the float. Gage led Taylor's horse and loaded it into the float and secured the door. He picked up some of the junk she had piled near her car, trying to help her and she snatched it from his hand, losing her footing and falling to one knee. Gage reached down to help her.

"Don't fucking touch me".

Gage stepped back. He looked across at Katie. She tried to give him an encouraging smile. With the final bag loaded Taylor got in her pretty white Mercedes and drove away.

Katie walked happily down the tyre track back towards the stables. Jan had made more progress than she could ever have hoped. She could now touch her all over, pick up her feet and put a halter on her. Katie felt proud not only of Jan but of herself. She had never been around horses until coming here, seeing Jan and the trust they had built together gave a lightness in her step that she had never had before.

"Where have you been?"

Katie let out a startled scream hearing Gage's voice. He stood in the paddock with the donkeys, she didn't even notice him until he spoke. The realization of having to make up a story on the spot soon set in. She tried to defer the conversation.

"What are you doing in there?"

Gage, however, wasn't fooled. He stepped one leg at a time through the lower rails of the fence and stood in front of her with his arms folded. Katie folded hers back, it felt like an old western movie face off.

"You didn't answer my question?". Gage looked intently at her, searching the expression on her face for any weakness.

"You didn't answer mine?". She just stood there smiling at him. Pointing her finger at him, she couldn't help but focus on the five little ass faces staring at them between the rails.

"I asked you first?". She could see that quick wit all over his face, he was enjoying every minute of toying with her.

"I was just out walking". It was simple and an easy answer. Gage glanced back down the track she had just appeared from. Raising an eyebrow, he smiled and laughed.

"So, it's your turn". Katie moved her hands to her hips, the cheesy grin on her face had him laughing.

"You were the one who said they made your heart feel happy, I was just seeing if it was true". Gage started walking back towards the stables.

Katie was surprised that he remembered what she had said all that time ago. "Well?" she called after him.

Gage stopped, turning back to her. The sunset gave a golden glow to his skin that nearly put her on her knees.

"Well what?"

"Did they make your heart feel happy?". She walked slowly towards him until she was so close, she could smell his cologne, looking up at him, hands childishly on her hips, waiting patiently for an answer.

He smiled, her innocence and the way she was so carefree around him now made him feel at ease. She didn't seem to worry about her hair being messy or if her shoes were dirty, Katie found pure happiness just standing with 5 donkeys, that was something he admired about her. Gage almost felt like he was choking   up.

"Ok, yes they did".

Katie bounced around him booming with I told you so's. Gage laughed at her antics. It was the first time in a long time that he laughed and felt good doing so.

Katie pulled Little Jim into her driveway to see a lady sitting on her porch. She had never seen her before.

"Can I help you?". Katie walked up the porch stairs slowly. The lady had nursing scrubs on.

"Are you Katie Thompson?" Katie nodded. The woman introduced herself as a nurse from Port Arthur Base Hospital. "We have been trying to contact you for a few days, the number we were given appears to be wrong, Endeavour Park gave me your address, its regarding Dorothy Watson".

Katie read the woman's name badge carefully, she was referring to Dot. "Yes, I know Dot, is she ok?"

"I'm afraid Mrs. Watson has passed away; you were listed on her medical record as being her emergency contact,"

Katie sat down slowly on the chair on her porch.

"She has family, um a niece, she works at the real estate and a sister here in town".

The nurse knelt in front of her. Katie didn't know what to say, what to do, she just sat there.

"That's correct, they have been notified and I'm sure arrangements will be made, can I call someone for you though?"

Katie stood and the lady hugged her before leaving. "No thank you, I'll be fine".

Katie watched her drive away. She got back in Little Jim and fought tears the entire drive back to Endeavour Park. She slid Little Jim into the end of the drive, stopping hard, sending gravel in all directions. Katie ran down the breezeway, as fast as she could she run. She cut across the grass instead of staying as she usually did on the tyre tracks. She didn't stop until she got to the rails of Jan's paddock slipping through into the long grass. Katie's knees buckled under her as she slumped onto the ground, her legs stretched out in front of her. The noise that finally escaped from her mouth was uncontrollable. Katie howled; legs stretched out on the dirt in front of her. She had never had a real best friend before, growing up in foster care she was always moved before she could get to know anyone properly. Dot was the first person she could ever truly say was a best friend. Dot knew everything about Katie's life, she never betrayed her confidence, she just knew Katie needed someone from the first day she met her at the blow hole, Dot just slipped into her life like she had always been there.

The grass rustled in front of her. Jan was slowly, step by step, getting closer. The beautiful blonde mare lowered her head, her good eye gazing down and sniffed her, wiggling her muzzle back and forth through Katie's hair. Jan softly nudged her nose against Katie's shoulder trying to get her attention, Jan could sense the devastation. Katie just cried, it was all she could do, a cry that came from deep in her soul, a moaning howl that she had no control over. Jan moved to the side and out of nowhere, without warning she lay down, sitting beside Katie with her legs tucked in front of her. She let out a deep groan, kicking her legs out allowing her body to roll onto her side, resting her head on Katie's leg. Katie wiped her tears, touching Jan's cheek, she closed her beautiful brown eye as she softly patted her face. Katie sat on the grass with Jan till the sun started to go down.

"Come on girl, it's time to get up". Jan with a few attempts to roll herself back stood up, shaking herself free of the grass and dirt. Katie kissed her nose. "I'll see you tomorrow". She walked back, following the tyre tracks like she usually did, to find Roy leaning against an old tractor hidden in the grass.

Katie jumped. "Roy, bloody hell, you scared me". He could see that she had been crying. "How long have you been standing there?".

Roy adjusted his hat and started to walk with her back towards the stables and smiled.

"Long enough".

Chapter 10

The clouds hung low and heavy, every now and then a few flakes of snow would fall, floating in the air gently before disappearing into the long grass. The air was eerily still, not a single breeze, not a sound, just silence. Katie arrived for work to find Nancy comforting Lily in the breezeway, Lily was crying. Roy stood outside the stall. Katie slowly walked closer, already feeling low herself, her heart sank deep into her chest, it was Clementine's stall. She peered over the door quietly to see Gage sitting cross legged in the centre of her stall her head cradled in his arms, patting her face as he gently talked to her. The vet had checked her one final time. He looked up at Roy, and to Gage and shook his head gently. Gage nodded back at the vet and removed his hat. The vet took a dark glass vile from his bag, filling up two syringes. Katie felt a lump growing in her throat. The vet administered the dose into the vein in Clem's neck. Gage talked gently to her.

"It's ok, my girl, go and find Kota, she is waiting for you".

Katie quietly cried. The vet watched Clem for a while as she closed her eyes before giving her the second dose. He listened to her heart, stood up and placed his hand on Gage's shoulder as he left him with her, just he and her, for the last moments. Gage was 6ft 6, a big proud man, who rarely showed emotion or spoke to anyone about his feelings, but Katie watched him sob uncontrollably stroking her face as she left. Roy walked back to the house with Nancy and Lily. The vet packed up his kit and left quietly.

Gage sat there, still stroking her face. The stalls were quiet, Leeroy watched through the wire from the next stall. All the inside horses were still. They all knew, like it affected them just as much as Gage. Katie opened the door of Clementine's stall carefully. She quietly sat down beside Gage. His hands still cradling her head. Katie gently patted her cheek and rested her hand on his, she could see now Clementine's broken Cannon bone, it was broken through the skin but wrapped in a light bandage. She didn't have to say anything to him, truthfully, she had no idea what she could possibly say to comfort him at that moment. He lowered his face to rest on her shoulder. Katie gently ran her hand along his arm. Roy returned a short time later, there was one last thing that needed to be done. They had to bury her.

"Is there anything I can do for you?"

Gage wiped his face with his sleeve. "Would you come with us?"

Katie nodded.

Gage lay a blanket over Clementine. The indoor stalls were uniquely built, they had a small door for the normal daily routine but in special circumstances the entire back wall of the stall that opened into the day run could open all the way. Gage unlatched the big slide bolts at the top and the bottom and pushed the wall open. Roy dismantled the day yard fence and drove the small forklift into the stall. Roy gently guided the forks under Clem, lifting her up. The stables still, like nothing Katie had ever experienced before, remained silent. The horses just stood quietly, but intently watching what was happening.

Roy drove Clem down the dirt road towards the donkeys, turning down the tyre tracks past Jan. Lily, Nancy, and Belinda walked behind Roy as he took her down into a small clearing between two tall gum trees. Katie took Gage's hand as they walked. He glanced down at her hand in his and smiled. Roy had already dug a hole with the excavator. Looking around at several crosses, Katie realized they were in a cemetery. Nancy said that many family horses and animals were buried here over the years. She wiped a tear away as she read the name on the cross next to where Clem would rest, remembering that Gage had told Clem as she passed to find Kota.

"Who is Dakota?". Katie whispered to Nancy.

"Dakota was Clementine's sister, they were twins born here at Endeavour, they actually shared a stall, all their lives, the same one Clem was in till Kota passed away a few years ago".

Katie's heart broke that little bit more watching Gage remove the blanket and stroke her cheek one last time before Roy gently lowered her to rest next to her sister.

"Gage left Clementine in with the other horses after Kota went, they were always together, he couldn't bear the thought of Clem being on her own in the paddock without her" Belinda added.

Roy parked the fork and got back in the excavator and filled in the hole. Belinda, Nancy, and Lily started walking back to the main stables. Katie stood beside Gage and placed her hand on his back.

"I can stay with you if you want". Gage smiled at Katie as he reached for her hand holding it tightly.

"Thank you but I think I will just stay here a little while longer".

"If you need anything". She squeezed his hand tighter.

Gage without hesitation wrapped his arms around her. Any other time she would have flinched but not this time. She felt safe with him. She wrapped her arms around his neck. The embrace was warm, and his arms held her confidently. Katie smiled and didn't even think twice when she kissed his cheek. He looked at her with tear filled eyes. It was in that moment, for the first time, she truly 'saw' him.

The snow fell heavily that night. Katie sat cross legged in the single armchair reading, sipping a glass of Moscato, a crochet blanket that Dot made her over her lap. The last few days had been draining, so much had happened in such a short period of time. She was excited to see the snow falling, it was something she had never seen before. Fin was more than comfortable lying on his back with his legs in the air in front of the fire, unapologetically taking up all the space. Katie heard a knock at the door. She didn't even hear any cars pull up. She glanced at the clock, 9.56pm. Katie opened the door slowly, not sure what to expect at that hour. It was Gage, drunk, covered in snow and wet through. She opened the door, looking out curiously and not seeing his ute, just foot prints up the snow-covered drive.

"Did you walk here?", she asked incredulously. Gage was shaking. He was so cold; she took off his coat and draped it across the back of the dining chair to dry.

"I walked from the pub". His voice was shaky. Katie was mortified.

"You walked from the pub" Katie repeated in disbelief. The hotel was at least a 5-kilometer drive along the highway. "Well, I hope you're not shy because you need to get out of these wet clothes".

Gage didn't care too much. The alcohol was keeping him warm on the inside, that's for sure. She wasn't going to take no for an answer, getting him a blanket from the hall cupboard and not so politely moving a very disgruntled Fin from in front of the fire. She hung his Jumper, shirt, socks and jeans on the clothes horse. As she pegged them on, she couldn't help but look over at his chiselled chest in the glow of the fire, she had never seen him without a shirt before, he had a decent amount of brown chest hair that gathered across just the top half of his torso and lightened as it got lower. He sat on the floor cross legged with the blanket around him in nothing but his boxers. Fin took no time in settling in the small space between his legs and the fire, that cat wasn't sharing with anyone.

"I'll make you a cup of tea".

Fin purred as Gage scratched him behind his patchy haired ear, he rolled onto his back inviting him to stroke his belly.

Gage smiled. "He certainly is confident isn't he". Gage smiled listening to him purr.

Katie passed him the hot cup of tea and sat back where she was before.

"So, where is your ute?"

Gage held the cup in both hands so it would warm his fingers.

"It's at the pub, probably wouldn't be a good idea to drive it home". Gage wasn't completely drunk, but he had definitely had too many to drive. "Thankyou for today". Gage scratched Fin's ear. The cat wasn't shy at all, stretching himself out as far as he could in front of Gage to hog the fire.

"I didn't really do anything".

Gage didn't move, just turned his head.

"You did more for me today than anyone else there".

Katie knew what he meant. It was being there emotionally, not having to say anything to make a difference, just holding his hand when he needed someone was something he cherished.

"I really am sorry about Clem, I am going to miss her," Katie felt awkward. Gage sat in front of her, pretty much naked. She felt the anxiety creeping up on her. She was starting to have feelings towards him, feelings she had never really felt before, true genuine feelings.

"Think it's time you talked to me". Gage locked eyes with her and she pulled away from his gaze quickly.

Fumbling with her words she had to think of something. Maybe Roy told him she had been spending time with Jan.

"What do you mean?" Katie kept it simple. She wasn't sure where this was going.

Gage reached for his phone, ran his finger over the screen a few times and passed it to her. It was the text message she sent him saying she wasn't scared of him, and he was asking her if she would tell him about it one day. Katie could feel the colour drain from her face; shivers ran down her back. He had shown her a vulnerable side today, but could she trust him enough to return that vulnerability. Rick was dead after all. She just looked down and played with a loose strand of wool nervously. Gage watched her become more and more uneasy.

"It's ok if you don't want to talk about it."

Katie relaxed a bit that he didn't seem to push her into talking about her past. The only one who knew the full story was Dot. She walked into the kitchen and bought a full bottle of Moscato back to her chair and poured a glass. Gage stood up and sat on the lounge across from her under the blanket. Fin, taking full advantage of the newly vacant floorspace, rolled back over onto his back.

Katie downed the glass and poured another. "When I was a child, I was taken from my mother and put into foster care, not just one home but several". She started.

Katie talked for an hour, Gage didn't move, he just listened. "I met Rick the day after I turned 19, he offered me a room to rent at his house and a job, at the time I didn't see anything wrong with it, he seemed like such a nice guy, but it didn't last", she continued with the story, ditching the glass and swigging straight from the bottle. She spoke about having to plan to escape, how Rosanna helped her and the night that she left.

"I arrived here and found the job add in the supermarket and texted you, I guess from then onwards you know the story, Dot helped me get this house, I owe her so much,"

"I knew Dot well, I'd like to come to her service with you on Tuesday, if you don't mind that is."

Katie smiled.

Gage looked at her seriously. "What do you want now? I mean what do you see for yourself?"

Katie lent back in the chair. "I just want to be happy, for the first time in my life I have everything I have ever prayed for, even the mangled looking cat,"

Katie looked at the clock. It was 2am. "If you want to go home, I can drive you, or you could stay here if you like". Katie's stomach knotted as the nerves crept back in looking at the near naked horseman on her lounge.

"If its ok, I'll stay".

Katie went to get him a pillow and another blanket. She watched him from the hallway cupboard, he stood up, dropping the blanket on the lounge walking across to his clothes in just his boxers. His back was perfectly muscular, in the warm light of the fire his skin glowed. For a moment she found herself holding her breath. Gage pulled on his now dry shirt. She put the pillow and blanket on the arm of the lounge.

"Is there anything else I can get you?" Katie stood still, just waiting for him to say something, watching him spread the blanket out on the lounge and walk around to stand in front of her.

"I'll be ok, thank you for trusting me with your story, that was brave of you".

The moment of awkward silence drifted between them as he looked down at her, she could feel her heart beating nearly out of her chest as he lowered his head and kissed her on the cheek. Katie swallowed hard, doing everything in her power to not lock eyes with him, she felt it from her head to her toes, she wanted to kiss him. She took a deep breath.

"Good night". She whispered, walking down the hall to her room.

Chapter 11

The snow had settled heavily overnight. Katie woke to look outside to a deep, sparkling blanket of white. Katie squealed loudly with delight, launching a sleepy Fin into the air. Hitting the ground running with hair standing on end, he took off into the bathroom trying to escape the screaming nutcase coming down the hall. For a moment, Katie forgot Gage was sleeping on the lounge. She came bounding into the loungeroom laughing and excitedly jumping up and down just like a child on Christmas morning in front of the window. She held a carrot in one hand and a small black top hat in the other. Gage, sleepily with one eyebrow raised lay on the lounge watching her.

"Ahh, everything ok?" He couldn't help but laugh at her, she wore hot pink tracksuit pants, a blue pantalette shirt, yellow scarf, a green beanie with a big pom pom on top and a pair of gumboots that had flowers on them. Katie spun around, suddenly remembering she had a house guest.

"There is so much snow outside, I'm going to build a snowman", She couldn't contain her smile. Gage sat up looking at her in more detail.

"In that outfit?" He laughed.

"Of course, come on, get up, let's go".

Gage watched her bounce out the door in a rainbow outfit of happiness. He got dressed, pulled on his dogger boots and peered out the front door to see her laying on her back in the middle of the front yard moving her arms and legs from side to side making a snow angel. She stood up clasping both hands in front of her with such joy he couldn't help but want to be a part of it.

"Ok, have you ever built a snowman?". He broke a long stick in half for the arms.

"This is the first time I've really ever seen snow".

Gage knew this moment was important to her, he remembered the first time he saw snow. Gage walked down the driveway, holding her hand as she skipped along behind him in her crazy outfit to the section of snow-covered grass at the very front of the house. He started to roll a small ball; he pushed it along the soft, fluffy snow. The more he rolled it along the bigger it became. He pushed it the entire length of the lawn and back, revealing a long avenue of grass, stopping it next to the letter box.

"Ok, now we need to roll another, you can start this one". Katie jumped into action. She started rolling the body, as Gage rolled the head. He lifted the second ball onto the first and then the third smaller one onto the top. Katie placed her little black top hat on his head and pushed the carrot into the centre for his nose. Gage pushed the sticks into the sides for the arms.

"It needs eyes". Katie looked around finding 2 black rocks, putting them in place. "Oh, hang on I forgot one very important thing". She wobbled up the driveway, keeping her feet in the footprints to the porch. She reached in the door trying not to get snow inside before coming back down the driveway with the same duck-like waddle carrying a red tartan scarf. She wrapped it around his neck.

"Oh, he is just gorgeous, let's call him Jack" Katie proclaimed loudly.

Gage couldn't help but smile. Her enthusiasm for life was infectious, it had been a long time since he had felt so carefree, she was bringing out that fun and happy side of him he almost forgot existed. Gage patted the side of Jack's face smoothing it out when suddenly a snowball flew past his face followed by a gasp and giggle.

"Oh, you didn't just throw a snowball at me?" As the words left his mouth another, with more direct aim, landed in the centre of his chest. "It's on!"

Gage bent down, picking up a handful of snow and shaping it in a perfect ball. Katie took off, wobbling across the lawn giggling. Gage followed her footsteps like a fox stalking his prey. His heart raced as he slowly peered around the corner of the house... 'whack' ...another ball hit him on the back of his head. He spun around to see her running back along the wall and around the corner. Maybe he was approaching this the wrong way. He thought carefully, filling an empty black, plastic, nursery plant pot full of ready-made snowballs, he walked following her footsteps along the house, positioning himself back against the side of the porch and waited. It was only a matter of time before she would come again with more snowy ammunition, this time he would be ready for her. He sat quietly. Not a sound, he felt a giddy excitement flow through him he had not felt since he was a child. A few minutes had gone by before he heard her coming up beside him, he was still out of sight, he kept his back to the wall and held his breath. He sat there watching her come into view. He could almost touch her, she was so close, but her scarf was so high up her face it blocked her peripheral view. She walked past him. He stood up slowly taking two snowballs from the pot and as he raised his arm to throw them, he knocked a pot plant sitting above him on the porch. She spun around and launched a snowball which hit the wall behind him. He laughed, throwing them back at her as she ran. He ran after her, catching her, picking up a handful of loose snow and rubbing it across her face. Katie laughed so hard she slipped over, grabbing hold of Gage's coat, dragging him down with her. They lay in a thick patch of snow laughing. Katie laughed so hard that her stomach hurt. Gage, legs straddled across each side, held her hands down at her sides.

"Do you surrender?" he said in a pirate like accent, laughing. He just smiled as he picked the little clumps of snow off her face. Gage pushed her wet, snow-covered hair off her cheek. The moment seemed to go in slow motion. He touched her jaw gently, leant down, and kissed her softly, his lips against hers were warm. Before she got a chance to say anything, his mobile phone rang. He smiled awkwardly, pulling his phone out of his pocket.

"It's Mum, I should take it".

She nodded, her heart racing a million miles an hour. He stood up and answered it, helping her up to her feet. She brushed herself off and walked back to the house, she could feel her cheeks burning, what had just happened? She slid off her gumboots and went inside. Gage came in shortly after, took off his boots and stood beside her.

"Dad's in town, he is coming by soon to pick me up to go get my car". Gage felt like he was letting her down by going home, especially after what had happened between them. "Thank you for letting me stay last night". He reached out and touched her hand, entwining his fingers with hers. He wanted so badly to kiss her again, the overwhelming pull he felt towards her was scary, something he never thought possible.

"I had so much fun this morning, thank you, oh and just so you know, there is no way that I'll ever surrender". She laughed nervously as he gripped her hand tighter.

"Would you have dinner with me?". A rush of nerves filled her body. She nodded. He turned to face her, tucking a strand of hair behind her ear just as a beep sounded out the front. He leaned down and kissed her cheek. Katie smiled as he started to walk towards the door still holding her hand, he didn't let it go, he stepped back to her as she looked up into his eyes, cupped her jaw with both hands, he slowly pressed his lips to hers as the horn sounded again.

"See ya".

Katie didn't have anything suitable for a funeral. In this weather she wasn't going to be able to drive too far so she decided to take a snow driving adventure to the small Op shop in Eaglehawk Neck. She had never driven in snow before, luckily the road had been driven on quite a lot that day, so she had a path already carved out for her. It wasn't as scary as she thought but rather exhilarating. The Op Shop was open, thank goodness. Katie looked through the racks. She didn't have any idea what to wear. The newspaper obituary asked mourners to wear something purple as it was Dot's favourite colour. There was a black, just below the knee, tight dress that would work and just like Dot was looking down on her she found a deep purple knee length coat. It was an outfit that was out of her comfort zone. She didn't dress up often, she never wore dresses, she didn't even own a dress till now but, in her heart, she knew this was the right one. She found a new pair of stockings and some low heels to finish. She was quite proud of herself. As she climbed back into Little Jim with the bag, she realized it was the nicest outfit she ever owned.

Katie put the dress and coat on hangers after giving them an iron, she was asked to do a reading at the service and practiced it several times in the bath. Fin announced his arrival loudly as he walked into the room demanding his dinner.

"Well, good evening to you too". She smiled as she opened the pantry door. His eager complaining became louder and louder as she found a tin of food. "Calm down, you're not going to vanish into thin air".

Fin obviously thought he would pass out from hunger at any moment, pushing himself against her legs back and forth yelling at her. "Ok here you go, jeez". She put his bowl down, he noisily ate his dinner. Katie wasn't very hungry, she found herself pining a bit for Gage. It caught her by surprise, feelings fluttering around giving her butterflies. She looked at her phone.

"No, Kate don't message him". She opened the fridge, then shut the fridge. She opened the pantry, then shut it. "Oh my god". She said loudly, frustrated with herself. She didn't know what she wanted to eat. So many options but nothing tempted her. She opened the fridge again. She took bits and pieces from the fridge and the pantry and made a grazing plate with cheese, salami, ham, and crackers. Putting another piece of wood on the fire she sat in the single armchair with Dot's blanket in her lap, watching the fire. She looked up again at her phone sitting at the coffee table. Finishing her plate, she let out a loud sigh. She couldn't stop thinking about the kiss.

"Ok, Fin, I'm going to bed". Katie pulled the covers over her shoulders and snuggled down as far as she could with a persistent fur ball demanding his share of the electric blanket. So many things ran through her mind. "Maybe I'll feel better in the morning." She said as Fin started to purr.

Chapter 12

Katie looked at herself in the mirror. She looked very sophisticated. The purple coat sat just above the hemline of the dress. It was a battle trying to get the black stockings on, but she managed it without putting a finger through them. The pointy toe heels made her legs look long. She felt confident but at the same time she felt completely naked, she never wore dresses, rarely even skirts. She was the jeans and boots kinda girl, so this was a big step out of her comfort zone. She put her hair back in a loose bun, little pieces framing her face and a black pair of drop earrings. It was important to her to look good today as much as it made her feel uncomfortable, she had to do it for Dot. She had to be confident when she felt like all she wanted to do was become invisible.

The service had pretty much the entire town present. Dot was well known and lived in Eaglehawk for over 50 years. She pulled Little Jim easily into the church car park. There was one good thing about driving a little car, she could park it in places most couldn't fit into. Gage waited for her at the base of the stairs where the hearse was parked. He wore a black suit with a purple tie and his grandfather's cufflinks. Gage watched her walk towards him, fixing her coat, arranging the collar nervously, she was regal in the deep purple coat and unexpectedly took his breath away.

"You look amazing". He beamed with pride, kissing her on the cheek. Gage, holding his arm out for her to link hers through and escorting her up the stairs into the church, didn't go unnoticed. Taylor sat on the row next to the door with her parents. Katie felt like everyone in the room turned their heads to watch them come in. Gage didn't waver one bit, he was a complete gentleman, Katie was admired from every corner of the room as she walked in with him. Dot's niece, Amy, approached Katie in the aisle, directing her to the front set of reserved seats.

"Will you sit with me?". She asked nervously.

Gage nodded, taking her hand, he led her to the front of the church, passing Dot's coffin at the front, it was covered in gum leaves, white roses, and white daisies. Her favourite flowers.

Taylor watched as he led her to the reserved seats. Her lips pursed tightly as the rage built inside her. Gage let Katie sit down, undoing his Jacket button he sat beside her. Nancy, Roy, and Belinda sat a few rows back as well as Louise who she met at the Lufra Hotel. Roy smiled approvingly, watching his son proudly sit with Katie.

It wasn't long before the family procession started. Katie's hands shook, Gage could see the program in her hand trembling. He reached over and grabbed her hand, squeezing gently. She looked at him, she was pale, the nerves rolled around like a washing machine in her stomach. Katie had never been part of a funeral, and she wanted to get it right, so many people were here watching. The celebrant started the service with a prayer. She introduced the first reading, read by Katie Thompson. For a moment she hesitated, looking back at the many faces looking at her, Gage squeezed her hand again, giving her a comforting nod. She stood up and walked gracefully to the lectern. The clouds shifted outside, a faint beam of purple coloured light bounced through the stain glass window, spanning brightly across the gasp filled room, resting on Dot's coffin. The nerves slipped away, and she smiled looking down at the purple light in front of her, she read confidently from the program, pausing where it was needed. Her composure was impeccable, maybe it was Dot was helping somehow.

Katie folded the paper and walked back to her seat. Gage smiled at her. "She is proud of you" he whispered. In that moment she felt an overwhelming sadness. Dot was her first best friend. Dot listened to her, comforted her and was the first real mother figure she ever had and the realization of losing that was setting in, even though she only had it for such a short time.

The service concluded after an hour. The coffin was walked out to the hearse, and one row at a time, the mourners followed. Gage took Katie's hand as they walked down the centre aisle and outside. People gathered on the lawn outside. Katie stood with Nancy, Roy, and Belinda and was stopped by so many people she didn't know to give their condolences and to talk to her about the amazing purple light while she was reading. Taylor and her parents spoke to Dot's family, Taylor in a black tailored suit, no sign of anything purple, strutted over to Gage and attempted to hug him. He didn't flinch or return the gesture, instead pushing her away. Taylor with no compassion for anyone other than herself looked Katie up and down, leaning in closer to her.

"You'll never be good enough for him".

Everyone within ear shot heard her. Nancy and Roy braced for the worst. Gage put his hand on the small of Katie's back as a sign of composure. Everyone was watching, what she did now would reflect the person she had become since being in Eaglehawk, the person she was becoming was confident, knew her worth, and above all, was strong, it wasn't worth it, Taylor just wasn't worth it.

Katie looked her in the face as Taylor smugly waited for a reaction, Katie simply smiled at her and said, "Thank you for coming today."

It took every inch of her self-worth to not react even though deep down the comment really did hit home. Was she really good enough for him? They were not together, so far it was just a kiss, but it played on her mind from that moment on. One after another she hugged and shook hands with people she didn't know, who wanted to know her. The feeling eventually became overwhelming. The hearse pulled away followed by Dot's immediate family.

"I should take the car home". Katie felt silently defeated and hurried towards the carpark in an effort to get away. Gage excused himself from his parents and friends and followed her.

"I'll come with you". Gage knew there was something wrong. Katie walked ahead of him; she didn't look back at him. "Are you ok?".

Katie, pulling off the purple coat like it was choking her, stopped as she reached Little Jim and turned, stopping him before he could say anything.

"She's right, I'm just not good enough for you". Katie was on the brink of having a big cry, she could feel it coming. She didn't say anything just quickly opened the driver's door, threw the coat onto the passenger seat and started the engine, foot down and sideways out of the carpark she took off. Gage desperately ran to his ute to go after her.

Gage skidded into 'I don't give a doo dah's' driveway after her. The snow man was still beside the letter box. She got out, leaving the driver's door open, and started walking quickly up the driveway, carrying the purple coat. Gage got out of the ute running after her, catching her halfway up the drive in a tight embrace, she pulled herself free from his grasp, continuing up the porch steps. Katie fell through the door as her emotions took over. Sitting on the floor in the lounge room she finally let it out, he sat down slowly on the floor in front of her as she lowered her head into his arms and sobbed.

She looked up at him, in her agony, he saw nothing but how truly beautiful she was, and he just couldn't hold himself back, he kissed her. Looking at him with tear filled eyes, after a moment, she kissed him again, it was deep. Suddenly, passionately, the moment seemed to speed up into fast forward. He pulled her closer, her legs wrapped around his waist, leaning him into the side of the couch, knocking the side table over spilling the metal box and contents onto the floor with a sudden crash, startling Fin sleeping on the couch, who took off running down the hallway in shock. The purple coat fell to the floor as he kissed her. His tongue rolling around hers. The heat between them burned strong. He tried to unzip her dress, but the zipper became stuck. She unbuttoned his shirt, and reached down to unzip his suit pants, revealing his erection. She pulled the tie from his neck, throwing it into the back of the room as he kissed her neck. It was intense, he breathed hard looking into her eyes, not shifting his gaze, not once, he ripped a hole in her stockings, pulling her underwear to the side, he pulled her closer to him, pushing his cock inside her. She could hardly breath. Grasping handfuls of his shirt, he pushed her harder against the side of the couch, her legs still wrapped around his waist she sat deeper onto him, rocking her hips back and forth as he came.

They sat holding each other breathing heavily. The realization of what had just happened was setting in. She sat with her legs still wrapped around his waist feeling him still inside her. She feared any words that could come out of her mouth now would surely sound wrong, she couldn't think of anything to say, the situation became awkward. She moved herself off him and stood up fixing her dress. Gage zipped up his fly and looked at the mess across the floor, hearing a terrified Fin wailing his contempt from the bathroom. They looked at each other and burst out laughing.

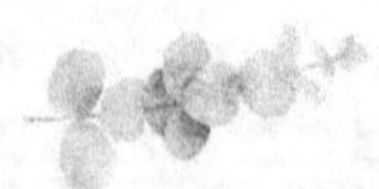

Chapter 13

Katie and Gage tiptoed around Endeavour Park like giddy teenagers. They were walking on a euphoric cloud. He found every chance he could to kiss her. He couldn't keep his hands off her. Lily dragged a big duffle bag across the carpark to the Endeavour Park Prado.

"What are you up to?". Katie asked her, curiously lifting the bag into the back of the car for Lily.

"We are going camping for a few days", Lily bounced around with anticipation.

"Where to?". Katie seemed intrigued. Lily put her headphones around her neck and her phone in her pocket.

"Just up the back paddock". Belinda loaded the last of the camping supplies. "Do you want to come?".

Katie smiled. She had never been camping before.

"I'd love to, but I told your Mum I'd work tomorrow while you guys are away". Katie watched as the family drove away. Katie finished feeding the horses and pushed the big doors closed for the night when her phone message tone beeped loudly.

"Need your help, can you meet me in the staff room". Katie sighed; she was looking forward to going home. The wind was picking up as the sun went down. She opened the door to find a red rose on the table on top of a large gold box. She opened the card. Put me on and meet me outside. Katie was nervous, opening the box, she unwrapped the tissue paper to find a pair of western jeans, a red collared t-shirt and the most beautiful pair of deep brown, embroidered Ariat boots she had ever seen. The pockets at the back of the jeans were also embroidered with a western detail. She hesitated but followed the instructions. She took down her hair, put her head down and ruffled her fingers through it to give it a bit of life. The outfit was perfect, the fit was on point. Taking a deep breath, she held the rose and walked out into the breezeway. Gage was leaning against Clem's stall door, like the leading man in a cool western movie. He was dressed in a pair of dark wash jeans, a green and white check shirt, white cowboy hat, and snip toe boots. His dimples were deep alongside that mischievous smile.

"What's going on?". Nervously she walked towards him, doing a little spin showing him the outfit.

"I thought I'd take you on a date, to the rodeo, if you want to go that is, you did say you would have dinner with me." Gage smiled, pausing to kiss her on the cheek. She looked adorable.

"Really, a date, I've never been to a rodeo," she clasped her hands together in excitement, exactly the excited, bouncy reaction he was hoping for.

Gage took her hand and led her outside, opening the door to a black Dodge Ram parked outside.

"Is this yours?"

He bowed his head, opening the door for her. "It doesn't come out much".

Just on dark, after an hour of driving, Gage pulled into Hilldale Showgrounds and parked the Ram. Hilldale was a small town that hosted one of the biggest rodeo and camp draft weekends in the state seeing hundreds come from all over Australia to compete and more to spectate. The main drawcard for coming to Hilldale was the two hundred- and fifty-thousand-dollar prize pool across all events.

Katie felt nervous and excited, there were so many people. The grounds were set up like show day, rides, food vendors, and grandstands around two arenas. The first one was named Bullside. The Bullside was home of the main rodeo featuring bulls, saddle bronc, and roping events. The second was called The Smoking Barrel, aimed at barrel racing and camp draft events. There was a main stage that was hosting a variety of competitions during the day such as Whip Cracking, Wood Chopping and Sheep Dog displays. Katie looked around like a kid in a candy store, she didn't know what to look at first. Gage smiled watching her so giddy. Everything about her was infectious, her innocent excitement and appreciation for little things inspired him, her newfound zest for life made him want to be around her all the time. He found himself not being able to get enough, a feeling he had not felt in a very long time.

Gage held out his hand. "May I hold your hand ma'am?"

Katie smiled, her face going red, all she could do was giggle. She took his hand as he led her around the amusements. There were fairy lights strung across the walkways between vendors. It was like a dream. She felt so proud walking beside Gage, him asking to hold her hand was everything to her. It may have sounded trivial to some people but to her that act on its own made her feel special.

Gage was well known and spoke to many people he knew; he introduced her to everyone. Katie could feel his hand tighten around hers. She looked up at him, the concern across his face was obvious as two men walked closer.

"Gage", one man with a black cowboy hat and big belt buckle nodded at him, he nodded back in return stiffly as they walked quickly past.

Katie glanced back over her shoulder to see both men watching them. "Who is that?"

Gage stopped at a food van, looking at the menu board, checking his watch, looking back at the menu. Katie looked back again to see two women had now joined them. One of them was Taylor. Katie's stomach dropped into her pretty new boots. Both ladies wore a Blue and White sash across their front that fastened at the hip with a fist size gold, star broach. Taylor and her friend looked fancy, sequin detail shirts, white jeans, shiny black boots, hats, and big blinged out belt buckles. The sash read Rodeo Queen Entrant.

"That's Will Aranson, Taylor's brother, he is a national champion bull rider, I didn't think he was going to compete after the fall he had late last year, broke both shoulders". Gage ordered two beef and gravy rolls, chips, and drinks. "Come on, let's go get settled for the main event".

Gage led Katie confidently into the grandstand across from the arena. They sat on the top row, high enough that they would be able to have the best view of the competition. A woman came out dressed in a red dress and sung the national anthem. The MC was standing in the middle with a microphone, introducing the bull riders that would compete in the nights final. Each rider was escorted out by a Miss Rodeo Queen entrant. Taylor escorted the top point scorer for the heats, Glen Rowley, and the other girl they had seen her with earlier escorted Will. There was 10 in total competing for the one hundred-thousand-dollar first prize.

Watching the riders was exhilarating. Katie found herself cheering loudly. He spoke to Katie quietly about the rules and what the riders had to do to score the highest points.

The MC announced the next rider as Will Aranson riding a bull named Blood Bath. The men standing on either side of the gate waited patiently as he tied his hand in place and settled himself into position. Will nodded and the gates flew open. Blood Bath certainly lived up to his name, he was rough, spinning fast one way before he threw his back legs up in the air and back around the opposite direction. The siren sounded for time, Will pulled the rope releasing his hand, sliding off, and running for the side rails. The crowd cheered loudly as he climbed the fence, waving at the crowd, he certainly knew how to work them, he was, after all, the crowd favourite for a reason. After several more riders, the MC announced a break before the top 5 riders would compete one last time.

"Would you like another drink" Gage asked her.

"That would be great, I might head to the bathroom and meet you back here."

Katie walked out of the toilets to see a group of people trying to pull two men off each other. Her heart sank when she realised one was Gage and the other Will Aranson. Katie saw Taylor standing with a group of Rodeo Queen entrants watching the fight. Will pushed him against the back wall of the bar, yelling in his face but she couldn't understand what he was saying. The desperation she felt was a deep burn through her stomach, she rushed across the road area between them, pushing through a group of by standers when she was suddenly tripped landing hard on the bitumen, her face taking the full brunt of the fall. The fight broke up instantly when she hit the ground. Taylor and her posse of blonde bimbo Rodeo Queens laughed at her, Will rushed towards his disrespectful sister ushering her and her friends away before security came, he still had to compete in the last round, if he was caught fighting, he risked being disqualified and it wouldn't look good for a rodeo queen entrant to be associated either.

A stranger helped Katie to her feet just as Gage reached her. A woman in the crowd had alerted the first aid tent at Bullside sending two medics to her assistance. Katie sat on a chair at the back of the bar. She had a laceration across her cheek leaving a flap of skin hanging down and grazed skin down onto her chin and neck. Her cheek was oozing blood heavily down the side of her face and onto her shirt. Katie touched her face, and looking down at her hand, started to panic. The medic placed a pad over the hanging flap to protect the wound, advising that he would send her via ambulance to the emergency room. Gage looked around for Will and Taylor as they loaded her into the ambulance. His blood boiled with their lack of concern. Will had been the one to start on Gage at the bar, he was defending his sister's honour, accusing him of moving on too fast with another woman, which is admirable, but Gage had done nothing wrong when it came to he and Taylor splitting up, he tried to talk calmly to Will when he pushed him against the wall starting a fight. They had simply grown apart. It was no one's fault. Taylor however played on the breakup to her family and friends making Gage out to be the bad guy.

He was angry and was trying hard to not let Katie notice his reaction. He kissed her forehead.

"I'll get the Ram meet you at the hospital". Katie nodded as the paramedic administered some pain medication into the canular he inserted into her hand, her eyes going glassy as the meds hit. Gage opened the home screen on his phone and called Endeavour Park.

A few weeks later, on a thick foggy morning, for her first day back to work, Katie pulled Little Jim into her usual parking spot at Endeavour Park beside a familiar white Mercedes. Katie was recovering well after the fall at the rodeo. She had surgery to clean the wound, the surgeon repaired the flap of skin leaving her with a scar across the apple of her cheek and quite a lot of swelling still on that side. It was still healing; the stitches had been removed and the surgeon assured her even though the scar was dark now, in time, as it healed more, it would fade. Gage didn't leave her side for the first week after surgery. He stayed at 'I don't give a doo dah' with her. They had grown so much closer since the fall.

Katie slowly got out of the car and looked around into the eerie, cold silence. It certainly seemed quieter than usual. Katie walked through the breezeway; all the horses were in their stalls still rugged. She stopped at the end of the breezeway and listened. She could hear people talking, peering around the door into the arena to see Roy, Gage, Will, and Taylor with a man she had not seen before. She couldn't hear exactly what they were saying. The man shook hands with Roy, passing him a folder of papers. Taylor turned her head to see Katie watching. She took a step forward putting her arm around Gage. Katie gasped, she couldn't control it, it just escaped from her mouth louder than she anticipated, she bolted as fast as she could. Gage, hearing the noise turned to see Katie running away, he pushed Taylor's arm away as she laughed. Will glanced to his sister with his disapproval. Gage knew what Katie thought she was looking at and it hurt him deeply because deep down he was starting to realise that he loved her.

"Seriously, Taylor, why do you have to be so cruel?" Gage signed the paperwork the man Taylor bought with her had.

"She isn't so pretty anymore". Taylor laughed as she saw Katie's face before she ran.

Roy put his hand on his son's shoulder as a suggestion to walk away. Gage just looked at her. Everything about her was cold. She got off on hurting people, the more she hurt them the better she felt about herself. They had been together since their late teens; she was never this way when they first met. Gage had watched her self-destruct over the years to the point where her hatred for life took over every ounce of her, no kindness at all, all she cared about was the Olympic glory. Looking at her with newly discovered hindsight he wondered how he stayed with her so long, their relationship had emotionally been over for a long time before it finally ended. Gage realised when he saw Katie run away that he had not been in love with Taylor for years, if anything, maybe a little, he now felt sorry for her.

Katie **led Sterlo** back to his stall and brushed him out, she didn't ride him that morning, just lunged him for a while. She secured his rug and fed him. He had lost a bit of weight since she started riding him every day. He sniffed around her pocket. She smiled reaching in and pulling out a chunk of carrot. Sterlo looked quite proud of himself as he took the piece from her hand.

Katie latched his door, picking up the donkeys' buckets of feed and started walking down to the back set of paddocks. The energy pull towards Jan's paddock was still there, it never escaped her, in fact it was stronger now than ever before. She tipped the feed into the furry vacuum cleaners' troughs and lent against the fence watching them honk at each other over who was eating from which side. Watching them, being around them still so many months after she arrived at Endeavour Park made her heart happy. It was easy to drift off into dream land around them, they didn't judge her or care what she wore or how she spoke, or the now scar across her face. They were always happily honking to see her. She watched a figure come up the path. It was Gage. She felt so confused. So much had happened in the last few weeks, as he approached, the nerves sank deeper in her stomach.

"Do they still make your heart happy?". Gage lent on the railing facing her.

Katie smiled and nodded, turning to look at him.

He looked tired, like the world was on his shoulders. "I owe you an explanation".

"Are you back with Taylor? Actually, don't say anything, it's probably better that you don't give me an explanation because then I won't feel like I'm not good enough, now that I look this way. I wonder if you will ever see me the same again,". Katie rambled and started walking back to the stables without giving him a chance to respond. She didn't want to hear the 'I'm sorrys'. She had worked too hard on herself since arriving in Eaglehawk to react. She felt disappointed, for allowing herself to have feelings, for letting him in, looking down towards Jan's paddock she stopped, in that moment she knew she had come too far to just walk away and keep the peace.

Katie turned around. "Actually, you know what, I am good enough, even if now my face is scarred and ugly, I won't let you or anyone make me feel like I am not worth taking a chance for, I have spent too many fucking years of my life feeling sorry for myself and hating my life, I am not that insecure, scared girl anymore, Gage, if you want to be with her that's your problem, but do me a damn favour, don't give me explanations".

Gage was speechless, he watched her turn and walk back to the stables.

"Wait", Gage ran after her, grabbed her arm turning her around to face him.

Katie pulled her arm from his grasp.

Gage put both of his hands up. "I surrender, give me a few minutes, please, Katie".

Katie sighed, folding her arms again waiting patiently for what he had to say. Gage led her to the old tractor Roy was leaning on that day he was watching her in Jan's paddock, motioning her to sit down.

"Taylor has a sponsorship contract with Endeavour Park, she has the Olympic team Dressage trials soon, we are still under contract with her, Will bought their solicitor, until the contract is up, we have to allow her access and give full support to her at the trials, she is threatening to sue". He desperately tried to explain to her. Katie stood up. Gage looked defeated, he reached out again to her hand, she stepped back, putting both hands in her vest pockets. Katie looked towards Jan's paddock searching for something to say. Why was she even so upset, they were still, after everything, not really officially together, even though every day it was implied, even after everything that had happened, he truthfully didn't owe her anything. Katie felt confused, hanging her head staring at the ground, sitting back on the tractor wheel.

"I'm not back with her," Gage stepped closer to her, he knelt in front of her, slowly lifting her chin so he could see her face.

"I am falling for someone else, Katie". Gage cupped her jaw in his hands and kissed her gently. His lips were warm, he touched her scar with his thumb.

Without warning, just like they knew the right que to come in on, all five donkeys started an out of tune chorus of honking. Gage laughed, turning to see all five of their nosey heads between the rails, voicing their opinions. He smiled at those 5, big eyed faces, kneeling in front of her.

Chapter 14

Before the sun rose, that glittery moment the sun started breaking through the trees, the gentle sound of walking horse hooves bounced around the crisp still air. Katie breathed deep, the air was fresh, almost stinging her throat it was so cold. She led Jan back down the grassy tyre grooves towards her paddock. Katie opened the gate, sliding off the halter, giving her a rub down. Katie had been riding Jan in the arena every morning for the last month, before the sun rose, before anyone arrived at work, no one knew but her and Roy. It was Roy's idea, she was the only one since his father to have this amazing relationship with Jan, it was something that Roy knew his father would have loved to have seen. Jan and Katie had built an amazing bond, Jan trusted her. Roy had been getting up at 4am every morning to teach Katie to jump Jan, just like his father dreamed. Jan was such a big mare that, at first, Katie was scared, but the trust and loyalty they had was the key. Jan trusted Katie completely. Katie could lead her into a raging fire, and she would follow her. Roy sat at the upstairs window every morning, instructing Katie. With each morning her confidence became stronger, and Jan's ability got better.

Roy packed up the poles while Katie put Jan back in her paddock. The secrecy of Katie training Jan was important, Roy was adamant about it, he knew that day he saw Jan lay down beside Katie that she would be the one that would change Jan's life. Nancy and Gage didn't trust her, when pop died, they wanted the horse to be put down because no one could get near her, they saw her as being dangerous, she could hurt someone. It took Roy over a year to achieve what Katie did in those first 3 weeks. Katie walked along the arena wall to where Roy was standing.

"How did you feel this morning?". Roy slid the last pole into the rack.

"It felt good, I am really proud of myself, she is getting easier to ride every day,"

"I want to talk to you about an idea, it's a bit risky though". Roy handed Katie a folded brochure. It was an entry form for a novice showcase that combined with the last round of Hobart Olympic Equestrian Trails. Katie looked confused.

"Hear me out". Roy could see the concern come across Katie's face. "The Trials are the end of the national level events, they have a jumping showcase for beginners who want to have a go at eventing, what do you think about entering you and Jan?".

"Are you bloody crazy?" Katie blurted out without thinking. "I am nowhere near a good enough rider for this".

"It's a novice meet; you don't have to be a professional, Katie, if you do well you can go on to the next events".

"You're forgetting something, how are we going to float Jan out of here, what will you tell Gage and Nancy?"

Roy smiled like he had an answer for everything. "We can take her a few days before, I'll think of something to tell them, it will give her time to settle once she gets there, you may just have to tell a few white lies with me to make it work".

Katie folded her arms. The idea was starting to grow on her. The family, representing Endeavour Park would already be in Hobart for the Olympic Trials.

"I wouldn't put you in this position if I thought for a moment, you or Jan couldn't do it, just think about it at least, you don't have to go on to compete further if you don't want to, but it will show you what I know you and Jan are capable of".

Gage stood in the carpark talking on the phone to the family of the riding school horses. Lily tried her hardest to eavesdrop on the conversation. Katie kissed Sterlo's nose, shutting his door, she joined Lily at the breezeway door watching Gage pace up and down, his face deep with concentration. He said goodbye and turned towards where they were listening. Lily and Katie took off down the breezeway. Lily held onto the wheelbarrow handles and Katie sat quickly on a hay bale trying to look inconspicuous.

"There will be a truck coming tomorrow morning to pick up these guys, another riding school has bought them, all except one".

"I'm going to miss them". Lily sighed.

Gage walked closer to Katie and handed her an envelope. She looked at Gage curiously as she opened it. She pulled out a contract of sale with her name on it as the owner. Katie started to tear up when she realised this was for Sterlo.

"Are you serious, he is mine?" Katie turned to look at the big, chunky, fella hanging his head out over the door, his goofy tongue poking out the side of his mouth, it was like he knew. Katie started to cry, she wrapped her arms around the big goof ball's neck. Gage smiled as he watched her, how happy she was. Without thinking twice, he reached out and placed his arm gently around her waist and kissed her on the cheek.

The family watched as the stockman loaded the riding school horses onto the transport truck. They were starting a new journey after 15 months at Endeavour Park. Sterlo nickered loudly watching them led out one by one. Leeroy threw his head into the air and let out a loud neigh as he passed Sterlo. Katie felt sad watching them all leave, she had got to know all of them well, maybe that was Leeroy's way of saying goodbye to his stable friend before being loaded on the truck. Cynthia was difficult as usual. She had a self-important air about her trotting down the breezeway. Katie couldn't help but think Taylor had embodied herself into her, the entitled attitude she always had, that attitude was certainly out on display today being the last loaded.

"It's funny how it can all just change in 24 hours", Katie mumbled watching the truck drive away.

She cleaned out the stables completely after they left. All the bedding was scooped into bins and taken away by Roy for compost. Gage pressure washed the stalls, spraying them down with disinfectant. Sterlo watched curiously through the wire, lowering his cheeky head down so only his eyes and ears were visible.

"I know you're there", Katie whispered, looking at him from the neighbouring stall. He nickered softly at her; it sounded almost like he was laughing. Katie watched him through the wire, laughing at his antics.

Chapter 15.

The nightly layer of fog was settling over the grass as Katie turned out the lights. The smell of sawdust pushed its way into every part of the building, it had become a comforting sense for her over the last few months. She felt safe, happy, and had come to know more and more about herself and who she was being here. The tack room light still on she looked back down the breezeway one more time, it was quiet except for the humming snore that came from Sterlo's stall. Gage watched Katie from a shadowed area just inside the first stall near the main doors. She smiled when she saw him watching her. She childishly walked towards him, her hands on her hips.

"Can I help you?".

Gage reached and took her hand, pushing Katie into the shadows, against the stable wall. His hands gently resting on her waist he kissed her, gently, his lips were soft and her knees near buckled as he moved his tongue over hers. Kissing up her cheek in little pecks, across her forehead and back down the other cheek. She giggled shyly. He made her body feel like it was on fire, a burning happy nervousness that started in the pit of her stomach and followed his hands around her body as he touched her. His kiss was passionate, she ran her hands under his t-shirt onto his warm chest. He turned her around, she leant forward, grabbing hold of the wire on the top half of the stable wall to support herself. Standing behind her, he ran his hand under her shirt and unclasped her bra, gently moving his hands around, he shifted her bra up to let her breasts peek out the bottom. Katie could barely stand up as he softly squeezed her nipples. The intensity had her unbuttoning her jeans as he did his, she couldn't wait. He pulled her slowly against him, his hands all over her body she let him slip inside her. The moment seemed to speed up. He reached his hand forward, moving her clit between his fingers as he pushed deeper and faster into her. Her legs quivered as he came, trying to be quiet, he didn't stop there, his fingers still moving quickly she buried her face into her arm to try and muffle the uncontrollable noise that came out of her mouth. Gage slowed down, she leant back against him, breathing heavily, he kissed her neck gently turning her around to face him a noise in the distance had them both sanding silently holding their breaths. They were not seen easily in the darkness of the stall. Gage buttoned his jeans quietly, watching for signs of movement. Katie quickly dressed herself, watching Gage edge quietly out of the stall and into the breeze way, edging slowly to where the noise had come from. He reached slowly picking up a stable rake, holding it in both hands he stepped around the corner before he let out a shocking yelp that seemed impossible to have been made by a Human. Katie saw a cat scurry past Gage off towards the tack room and she burst into hysterical laughter.

With the float hooked up, Gage drove Nancy and Lily to Melbourne a few days later to pick up a new horse for Lily. Lily wanted to start competing in junior events and needed a horse that would be capable to take through the levels. The new horse was named Big Ocean Lights but would be called Lightning on the daily. Lily was excited. They would be gone for a few days and Roy used this time to his advantage. There was only a month till the Olympic trials and so much to prepare for if Katie was going to jump Jan in the beginners showcase.

Taylor was going to be the problem. Roy had to be careful not to let her catch wind of what they were doing. Taylor trained in the mornings. Katie came in as normal and mucked out Sterlo's stable, fed the donkeys and the mares in the outer paddocks. Endeavour Park was quiet now the riding school horses had left, so Katie took advantage of the time, to get some cleaning done. Taylor walked around like she owned the place as usual, there was nothing positive about her, she looked at Katie with absolute disgust every time she saw her. It wasn't till mid-morning that she finally left. Roy started setting up jumps in the arena with the guise that there were some riding students coming out to use the facilities, so not to draw any unnecessary attention from Taylor.

Katie walked Jan from her paddock into the arena. Katie saddled her up, the nerves were settling in as she placed her foot in the stirrup iron and climbed up onto Jan's back. Roy had set out 7 jumps that morning, all various heights. Roy had them numbered and gave instruction on what to do. This was a basic run through of what she may get on the big day.

After training, Katie looked through the information Roy handed her about the beginner showcase. It read like it was to encourage more people to try the sport and by having a showcase of novice riders would give a peek into the sport for those who has never competed before.

The collection of stapled pages had everything Roy could think of that she needed to know. She wouldn't be allowed to look at the course until the day of the event. There would be 13 jumps ranging from 60cms to 1 metre at the highest. Jan had been jumping 1.2metres at training so she wasn't completely unhinged at the thought of the heights, but with each day that passed, her nerves sank deeper into her stomach.

Jan was starting to really find her stride with jumping. She was easy to guide over each set. Katie felt like the bond between them, and the trust Jan had for her was the key in her confidence. Jan was blind in one eye, so it was always going to be a challenge. As she came up to the jump, Jan would turn her head slightly to get a good look at it. Jan jumped so effortlessly now, it was almost like Katie didn't have to do anything, Jan just knew.

Katie watched the truck pull into the main drive and back up against the loading ramp. Gage told them Roy had been to the abattoir sales and they would be accepting four horses Roy had saved from the sales.

Four horses unloaded and were led into the inside stalls. Katie recognised one of them instantly, her heart fell into the pit of her stomach and tears fell from her eyes. It was Sherlock. The other three she had not seen before. There was one white and brown paint named Gringo, a chestnut mare called Twilight, a grey mare named Stormy, and Sherlock. Katie stood at his stall door in complete shock of his condition. He was severely malnourished, he had open sores across his back and his feet desperately needed a farrier. It seemed like not so long ago that he left, and the other school horses were sold and in such good condition and now here he was back again and in such horrible circumstances.

Roy often went to the abattoir sales, these horses in the pens were doomed for slaughter and each time he would have to drag himself away, most of the time not buying. Roy said he knew it was Sherlock as soon as he saw him, but he was in an auction lot of four horses, so he had to buy them all to get him back.

Gage, Nancy, and Belinda were so engulfed with the care of the new horses that they almost forgot to look around them. Roy may have bid on the horses at first because of Sherlock but it also gave him and Katie a shield to train Jan. Taking the focus away from their early morning training sessions and onto the new arrivals. Belinda took to Sherlock almost instantly, she used to ride him often when he was there with the other riding school horses. Gringo was going to need some work from Gage, he was scared and abused but not in bad condition, and with training could be rehomed, Twilight and Stormy were older brood mares, not ridable but beautiful ladies, kind and gentle like they knew they had been rescued, they would go out into the paddock behind Jan with a couple of retired race horses to simply enjoy life. Roy always had a soft spot for the older horses.

Chapter 16

Taylor watched Katie and Gage walk down the lane way from the donkeys, towards the arena holding hands. Taylor wobbled into the arena, she led her horse across the sand and tied her to the bailing twine. Taylor was drunk and angry. The jumps were set up, none of them were usable for her, the wrong height, wrong amount of space between. She started kicking the poles off the side rails and swearing.

Gage sighed heavily, kissed Katie on the cheek, leaving her to watch partially hidden from sight. It was starting to cloud over, a light misty rain danced in the air on the wind, he saw the wine bottle, empty in the top of her bag on the stairs.

"What's the problem?". Gage walked across the arena.

Taylor was picking the dirt out from under one of her perfectly polished fingernails.

"How am I supposed to train with the incompetence at this place?". She spat her insults at him with intention to get under his skin.

He had seen this behaviour from her so many times that he could almost predict exactly how it would flow.

Gage looked around the arena, he saw Roy standing up on the viewing platform quietly watching her.

"This isn't the best time to be out here, there is a storm coming in".

Taylor wasn't having a bar of Gage's apparent concern for her safety.

"What do you care anyway?"

Gage sighed and put his hands in his pockets, stepped in front of her so she couldn't get on her horse.

"Get out of my way". Taylor attempted to get past him, and he moved again to block her, she lost her footing and came to rest on one knee in front of him.

Roy walked quietly down the steps and stood beside Katie.

"We could have been something you know?". Taylor sobbed loudly, her nose running down her top lip. "We had it all, together our family names, we could be unstoppable in this industry".

Even though their relationship was over he still felt bad for what had become of her, she was the gold medallist hope for the coming Olympics, but she was struggling to cope with the pressure, more so, life in general. She had been lashing out at everyone who crossed her path.

"What do you want, Taylor?" Gage was trying not to feel sorry for her, that's exactly what she wanted, that's how she managed to keep the relationship going for so many years. She played on that empathy from him.

Taylor stepped forward and kissed him. His hands still in his pockets he stood there, didn't kiss her back, didn't react to her at all. Taylor pulled away and stared at him for a moment before she started laughing. Gage turned to see his father standing with Katie. He nodded his head towards them.

Roy and Katie started walking across the sand towards Taylor's horse, Enchanting Symphony, and quietly untied her. Katie found herself holding her breath the closer she got to Taylor.

"Seriously, her? You choose her over me? She is nobody, Gage, nobody,". Taylor wailed a pitiful, sobbing moan as she sat down on the arena floor in the sand.

"She is as scarred as that ruined horse she rides".

Roy's eyes grew wider at her words as Gage looked back at him for some kind of guidance. Did Taylor just give away everything they had worked for? Roy's stomach was churning looking up at Katie, as he led Taylor's horse from the arena. Gage was always so critical of Jan and how dangerous she was, if he figured out what they were doing it would be over in an instant. The look in his eyes though was hurt, Katie reached out to touch his arm to talk, he brushed it off walking towards Taylor, he didn't even look back at her.

Gage knelt in front of her and held out his hand.

"Come on, I'll take you home."

Gage never called Katie after taking Taylor home, he always called her before heading to bed. Not even a text. Gage left Endeavour Park the following morning without speaking to anyone. Katie and Roy worked Jan early that morning as they always did, Katie was quiet. Roy could see in the way she rode Jan that morning that she wasn't herself. Katie bought Jan around the outside of the arena instead of lining up the next jump at a slow walk.

"I'm sorry, Katie," Roy was genuinely worried. Katie stopped Jan at the gate and sighed heavily. The morning air felt heavy, the weight sat on her shoulders solidly, nothing she could do was going to shift it. Roy reached out his hand, holding a piece of carrot for Jan.

"I know my son better than anyone, it will be ok, he will come back".

"The way he looked at me, he knew what Taylor said was true, I dread to think, though, how long she had known what we were doing?".

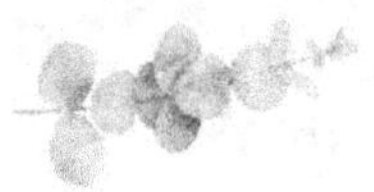

Chapter 17

Katie sat on 'I Don't Give a Doo Dah's' porch, a glass of wine in her hand, with crossed legs in a red pair of tailored pants, a neon yellow shirt covered in small, dog paw prints, a blue scarf, and floppy orange hat she crocheted herself that had a red flower pinned to the front. Katie liked to be different, she just put on what made her feel happy. Fin sat comfortably in a flowerpot sleeping, not caring much about the dainty, little yellow flowers flattened under his orange fluff. The sun was going down, sending a gentle coolness through the air, sending goosebumps up her arms. She stood up, looked at the big empty box filled with cut to shape foam pieces and plastic wrapping feeling quite proud of herself. The small 2 burner bbq she managed to build on her own was complete.

Looking down at the small, sealed individual compartments of the pre fab, building condiments, she counted 4 washers, 2 small screws, 2 large screws and a small silver metal bracket the size of her thumb she wasn't even sure was mentioned in the foreign language instruction booklet.

"Fin, surely these are just spares, do you think?". She said holding the packet towards a sleepy, unmoved cat.

Katie radiated pure joy and excitement as she jumped up and down on the spot admiring her work, who cares where the left-over screws went, it was standing and appeared to be solid. She darted inside, the screen door flying back against the external wall with tremendous force, startling Fin high off his dainty flowers and running down the yard at full speed, hair standing on end.

She came back out with a long metal tray, the door slamming shut behind her. She slid the tray easily onto the small side table on one side of her new bbq. There was oil, salt and pepper, tongs and a large piece of rump steak sprinkled with a garlic spice, covered with a blue and white checkered t-towel. The reality soon set in when she couldn't get the gas bottle hose connected.

In a fit of Aussie, wine infused, verbal rage, a rainbow of language flooded out of her mouth as she buried herself into the cupboard under the burners. By this point Fin, debating his chances for a free meal was sitting on the top step watching intently like a nosey, uninvited, self-appointed site manager.

"Stupid bloody, fucking thing, what the fuck, come on seriously, why won't you fit in the god damn, bloody, fucking hole?" She leant out of the small cupboard, her orange hat brim drooping down over her face, reaching for the Chinese instruction booklet to see Gage standing at the bottom of the porch steps. Taking a moment to gather her thoughts, she took a sip of her wine, pushed the floppy brim out of her eyes, so it stood upright from her forehead as the red flower fell off onto the floor.

"Hiiiii, I was just trying to, um, negotiate dinner with the bbq".

Gage couldn't help but smile. This is the one thing he loved most about her. She was quirky, didn't care if people were watching, she was going to be true to herself no matter what. She moved aside, without saying anything, sat down on the concrete and passed him the unreadable instructions. Gage knelt down to address the problem like any true Aussie man would. He looked back at the packet of left over hardware.

"Well, it's not connecting because you have the hose back to front, that silver bracket needs to screw in here, probably with these, to hang the gas bottle on", Gage said holding the packet of leftovers towards her.

"Pass me that screwdriver?". Gage used the two small screws and washers to secure the bracket to the side wall of the bbq and the 2 large screws and last few washers to secure the gas pipe connection into the burners of the bbq, in the designated holes. Fin pushed his way past to stand in the small cupboard space under the bbq where the gas bottle sat, watching Gage with a serious, unimpressed stare, inspecting the adjustments to the bbq fiasco.

"Ok, that's done, you now have to run the burner for a while to burn off the protective coating to the plate". Gage turned the tap around in the open arrow direction and put the burners on high. He looked down at her filling up her wine glass.

"I talked to Dad, he explained everything, I'm glad it's worked out for you two, you should be proud".

Katie took a long sip of wine; she could feel her eyes growing wider by the minute. She tried with everything she had to not look guilty or completely confused. She just tried to stay calm and act like she knew exactly what he was talking about. Looking down at the glass and back at him, she took another sip, holding it in her mouth for a while before swallowing. She needed to think carefully about what she said next.

"Do you want a beer?". She blurted out with a slight cough.

Gage nodded, picking up a determined Fin, putting him on one of the porch chairs out of the way as he fiddled with the hotplates. Katie casually walked inside and found her phone. She had no new messages. Texting Roy to find out what had happened she grabbed Gage a beer from the fridge and walked back out to the porch, owning whatever it was Roy had lied to his son about. Gage lent down and kissed Katie.

"So, you want to stay for dinner?"

Gage nodded. She rushed back inside to get a chicken breast out of the fridge and to check her phone again. No messages still. Pushing the door open she slid out trying hard to look and act normal.

"You can have the steak, I'll have this", she said sprinkling the chicken breast with some seasoning.

Katie had a nervous burn running through her stomach. Maybe it was better to just say nothing at all, keep the conversation neutral, avoid the mystery topic all together.

Dinner was cooked to perfection. Katie liked her meat slightly charred, more on the burnt side than under cooked. Gage smiled at her as she cut her Chicken.

"Is it cooked enough for you?". Gage smiled as he cut into his rare steak.

"Colour is flavour, I like lots of colour, yours is still mooing". Katie, a little drunk, laughed like a squeeky toy, a toot followed by a long drawn out laugh then finally a deep breath.

Gage finished his beer. Katie sat on the porch in front of Gage as they watched Fin chase a moth in and out of the darkness and porch lights.

"I never thought I'd see the day dad would let that horse go, I'm proud of you for helping him make that decision, it will be in everyone's best interest". Gage sighed. "At least that will give Dad something to take his mind off Taylor at the trials. Thank you for offering to help, Dad will need support when she goes, I'm not sure I am the person that can offer the empathy that you can".

Katie kept her eyes down cast. "The woman that Dad has given her to, I hope she knows what she is in for, he said you would go with him when he takes her to her new home".

Katie nodded.

"I better get home; I told Dad I'd check on Sherlock before I went to bed". Gage put his elbows on his knees and leant in and kissed Katie softly on the lips.

"I'm sorry about how hard it's been lately; I'll see you tomorrow." Gage touched her cheek with his finger softly.

Katie smiled holding onto his hand till the last moment before letting go and watched him get in his ute and drive away. She checked her phone. Still nothing from Roy.

Katie pulled Little Jim into the driveway feeling nervous. There were no other cars, the stables seemed quiet except for Sterlo's whinnys when he recognised her footsteps in the breezeway. Lily came running down the breezeway bouncing around hardly able to contain her excitement.

"Look, Katie, look, I'm going in my first competition, Gage entered me in it", Lily handed Katie the information pack that had arrived in the mail. The Hobart Equestrian Association, Novice Showcase. Katie felt almost faint.

"That's amazing, Lily", she exclaimed, handing the folder back to Lily who scampered off towards the house, looking back to see Gage standing in the doorway smiling.

"That's exciting, a showcase". Katie said struggling to hold herself together and act normal.

"Yeah, it's a special feature to the trials, more like a display for new eventers wanting to get going, they have prize money and trophies though, but slightly different rules, the top 3, I think the info said, get automatic entry to go into the first round of events for the new season so it will get her started anyway, I'll catch you later, have to head into town". Gage kissed her on the cheek, Katie swallowed hard. It was one thing to be registered for the showcase but now the entire game had changed. Now she would be in it against Lily. Katie felt sick, she turned to see Roy pull up in the Endeavor Park ute. Katie was feeling exactly the same as the look on Roy's Face as he got out and they both walked together down the breezeway.

"I can't do this now, Roy, Gage is going to know as soon as he sees the list of participants, we may as well just call it now and forget the idea".

Roy chuckled to himself. Katie stopped and starred at him laughing.

"I'm not sure i could have wished for a better plot twist myself, this is a good thing".

Katie was mute, all expression fell from her face, hands on her hips as she watched Roy giggle to himself. "He won't know it's you until you ride out into the arena, you are entered under your real name remember, Abigail Thompson".

If the colour had not completely drained from her face before, it now was empty.

"Trust me, it's going to be fine". Roy just grinned at her, a cheeky, mischievous grin.

Chapter 18

The weekend of the trials came around quickly. How the whole secret hadn't come unravelled by now, Katie didn't understand. Taylor had left for Hobart earlier in the week with her brother, Will, and her coaches. Gage had loaded Lily's horse into the blue float early, before the sun came up, and left with Nancy and Belinda a few days before. According to Roy's elaborate hoax, Gage thought that Katie and Roy were taking Jan to her new home which Roy told them was on a property on the outskirts of Hobart on the day of the trials, but instead, Roy had booked Jan into the Ballington Stables that was located close to the Equestrian Centre the trials was held at.

Katie led Jan into the arena. Jan's mane was still neatly braided, and her clean, shiny coat was beautiful as the sunrise peaked into the arena. Katie brushed her down, feeding her a few carrot treats. Roy carried a big black bag, laying it over the rail, he unzipped it like a child on Christmas morning. It was a beautiful, navy rug. It had The Endeavour Park logo in gold on the side above her full name 'For the Love of January'. Roy pulled it over her back and fastened it at her chest and across under her, clipping into the hooks on the side.

"It's beautiful, Roy". Katie stroked Jan's face as she admired the rug.

"It's the one my father had made specially for Jan; this is the first time I've seen it on her". Roy sounded emotional as he cleared his throat, pulling out some padded travel boots for Jan's legs. It had been years since Jan had been in a horse float and to say Roy was nervous was an understatement.

Katie talked to her quietly as she led her down the breezeway to the float. Jan stopped and sniffed the float walls. Katie didn't realise how tall Jan was until she took that first step into the float. Jan looked back towards Katie as she closed the guide bar beside her. Katie talked to her, reassuring her that she was ok. The whole exercise seemed to go without drama. Roy and Katie hopped in the Endeavour Park four-wheel drive and the journey finally started.

The drive to Hobart from Eaglehawk neck was about an hour. Jan travelled quietly. You wouldn't even know she was in the back. Katie read through the information book again and again. Roy couldn't help but smile as she fidgeted. The trials were to be held tomorrow during the day and the showcase was in the evening. It was risky taking Jan the day before the event, a lot of horses spend a few days prior in preparation, but Roy wasn't taking a chance to have anyone see them too early. To Roy, this was a way to show his family that she wasn't dangerous, that Walter saw something in Jan, other than just a broken horse. For Roy, this was something he had to do for his father and for Jan. Katie had shown him, over the last several months, that Jan was indeed a sweet-natured horse dealt a cruel hand, Jan had come out of her shell, and it was all because of Katie and the bond she had with her.

Roy pulled the old red float into Ballington Stables. He was met by an elderly man who shook his hand fondly, Roy introduced him to Katie as Neville Parker. Neville watched as the door lowered and Katie walked into a nickering Jan who seemed relaxed and calm. Jan backed out of the float looking like a million bucks. Neville smiled softly, Katie stopped, and he held out his hand to her. Jan pushed her muzzle into his chest, like she remembered him.

"Katie, Nev used to know Jan when she raced, he owned the stables next to where she was kept."

Katie watched him stroke her face and look intently at her scar.

"I'll never forget the day Wally saved her, he loved her so much, boy, would he be proud to see her today".

These unique stables, now privately owned by Neville, were attached to the equestrian centre by a long grassy laneway. They were rarely used by competitors anymore as a more modern facility had been built to replace it. Roy, knowing the owner well, knew there would only be a few horses boarding there that were not involved in the Showcase. The story of 'For the Love of January' was well known. The day Walter Morgan beat the trainer within an inch of his life was one people still talk about. Despite going to jail for the assault, he was applauded for the actions he took. People had a lot of respect for Walter.

Katie led her into the beautiful old stables. The smell of the aged timber beams above was in a weird way comforting to her. She pulled off her rug and travel pads and brushed her down again. It was important to keep their heads down. The locals would recognise Jan, Roy was sure of it, so they needed to stay out of sight, they were, after all, supposed to be still at home.

Later that evening, Katie, Roy, and Neville sat in the dining room of the cottage near the stables. Nev recounted old stories about Walter and the trouble they used to get into when they were younger. It was nice to listen to the history that Nev remembered about the days when Jan raced.

"She was amazing, no matter what weight they put on her, she would just fly".

Katie excused herself and tiptoed across the grass to the stables to check on Jan. Jan was laying down, peacefully sleeping. Katie rolled out her swag in the empty stable next to Jan's. She felt in her heart that she had to stay close to Jan that night. She lay there, quietly imagining that this is exactly what Walter Morgan would have done. The earthy, woody smell was calming, listening to Roy and Nev's laughter, she slowly drifted off to sleep.

Katie woke to several missed calls from Gage. She called him back.

Prep had started on Jan early. They had cleaned and polished all the tack for Jan a few days before and packed them in the back of the car out of sight. All the prep for Jan had to be done that morning. Roy was finishing braiding the top third of Jan's tail when she came back in from talking to Gage.

"The trials have started; Taylor is doing well apparently". She said dryly.

"We will need to go over there soon and make an appearance; Lily is competing too so, we will need to go and check in on her as well," Roy spoke quickly. He was nervous. A lot had to happen to make the day possible. They both had told lies to Gage and the family in the hope that they may look past them when they see how much they have worked for this moment.

Neville handed Katie the day's program for the showcase. There was a simple run down of jumps. 10 in total. Each were numbered. Roy told Katie that because this was a special event they would run it a little different. There were 24 riders, each will do the course and the top 5 would come back for a jump off. The organisers thought it would be a fun way to get the crowd involved rather than a normal meet program.

"You are booked in to walk the course at 4pm, after the trials have concluded".

Katie bent down and painted Jan's hooves black, then undoing the braids in her mane, she combed them out to reveal a beautiful wavy look. Jan seemed relaxed. Maybe, she remembered her old racing days. Katie sprayed Jan's hind quarters with a diamond, quarter spray and took out her comb. She had been helping Lily with her horse practicing the marks she wanted. Katie went for a checkerboard pattern; it turned out better than she could have imagined. The multi colours in

Jan's coat and the high gloss shine from the diamond spray really set the little squares off.

Katie stood back and admired Jan who still seemed relaxed. Nev agreed to stay with Jan and get the last few things ready while they went over to the trials. Katie found Gage in the stands while Roy found Lily and helped her check over her horse ready for the showcase. Gage hugged her tightly. Katie sat down beside Gage who was looking at her closely.

"You look really nice today, I've missed you" he held her hand and she leant into him. The crowd was bigger than she anticipated. She suddenly felt physically sick, nearly to the point of needing to vomit. This was the crowd she was going to ride in front of soon. The media was set up along the side arena behind the wall. Many photographers were taking photos in various positions amongst the stands.

The arena was beautiful. Every jump had flowers alongside it, there was a water jump also. The presentation was Olympic quality. Katie noticed the jumps they were doing looked sky high. Taylor, she hated to admit, was impressive. She rode a clean round, no faults. Not a strand of hair out of place. Disgustingly perfect actually. Katie rolled her eyes.

Gage didn't ask about Jan, even when Roy joined them. Jan was a painful subject for him. He missed his grandfather, but to Gage, that horse was nothing but trouble. The final round was starting shortly. Katie could see Will Arranson and Taylor's family sitting in the front row. The whole Morgan family watched from the top of the stand as the first 14 riders completed the course. Taylor was next. She had had clean rounds so far. Kate couldn't help but cringe as she watched.

"On Enchanted Symphony, Taylor Arranson".

Her horse trotted out with the same impeccable level of self-importance as her rider. They went through clean until the final jump, Enchanted Symphony stumbled on the take-off, clipping the top of the jump sending the panel tumbling off onto the sand. The crowd gasped. Gage held his hand across his mouth. Taylor had 4 faults for the final round. Katie smiled, hiding her face with her hands as Roy clasped his fist. She wasn't sure if it was a sign of relief or resolve. Those 4 faults would have Taylor place 6th. The final decision if she made the team would be announced at a later ceremony, either way her sponsorship with Endeavour Park was now over.

"I better go get Lily ready for the showcase", Gage said softly, taking Lily's hand and leading her along the line of seats. He didn't give much emotionally; he didn't even say goodbye just walked away. In some ways it was an end to a painful chapter for him, much more than his family.

Only riders were allowed to walk the course. Katie walked back into the big indoor arena to find they had moved and transformed the jumps into the 10 she had been given that morning.

They looked so much different to what she had been used to with Jan. A few had cross bars, one was a small wall, and the rest looked like fences. Her lack of experience was shining brightly. 4 other riders had the same time slot as her. Katie walked the course; she kept her head down to try and hide herself from the crowd. Nancy and Belinda were sitting in the stands. Taking note of where the numbers were. All jumps needed to be in order, and she would be faulted for her horse balking, for her falling, per pole or fence down. Katie left quickly and walked briskly back to the Ballington Stables.

Jan was stunning. She was fully saddled and ready to go. Katie wore tan jodhpurs, a white, high neck shirt, black shiny knee-high riding boots, and a black suede helmet. Roy handed her a brown paper bag. Inside was a new navy coat with gold buttons embroidered with the Endeavour Park logo. Roy and Neville watched her put on the coat. They were like proud parents. She matched Jan beautifully.

"Ok kiddo, it's up to you now,". Roy gave her a big hug. "I'm really proud of you Katie, if only my dad could be here to see it".

Neville and Roy took their seats in the stand soon after Gage. Taylor and Will Arranson sat 2 rows in front of them.

"Where's Katie?". Gage muttered to his father. Roy smiled proudly.

"She will be here soon".

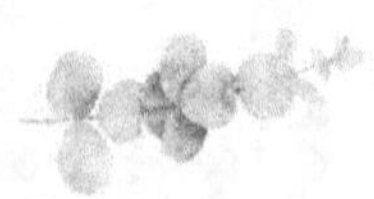

Katie drew number 16 for the order. Lily was 2nd out. Katie rode Jan down the grassy laneway into the waiting area outside the arena for riders. Jan was calm, she didn't flutter or faulter, she walked down the lane like she owned it. Lily watched as Katie rode Jan in, staring at her across the practice yard, slowly pulling up beside her, also wearing an Endeavour Park coat.

"Does my brother know about this?". Lily looked concerned as Katie shook her head. "I knew there was something going on all these months". Lily admired Jan. "She really does look amazing". Lily smiled and held her hand out to shake Katie's. "Goodluck".

Jan was the tallest horse and possibly the most beautiful in colour. Katie couldn't help but feel like everyone was looking at her. The scar on Jan's face was on the same side as Katie's. Her heartbeat was fast as the nerves really started to creep in.

It wasn't long before the MC started the showcase. Telling the audience what they were about to see. It was Lily's turn in no time.

"Riding her horse 'By the Ocean Lights', please welcome Lily Morgan."

Gage cheered loudly. The crowd fell quiet as Lily started her round. Lily went over all 10 jumps comfortably with only 4 faults from a pole falling.

3 more riders come and gone.

Katie sat waiting; Jan was starting to become a little bit jumpy. An older man with an earpiece motioned her and called for number 16. She moved forward towards him. The man looked carefully at Jan's face and back to the list of names on his board.

"Hi there, I have been watching you since the moment you came in, I know this horse very well, when I used to do farrier work years ago, I believe I did her feet".

Katie smiled. The knot in her stomach worrying what he was going to say slipped away.

"Goodluck today miss".

Katie felt concerned as the man walked away talking into the microphone pinned to the front of his jacket. Jan started to jump around; she was starting to stress. Roy couldn't sit still as rider number 15 left. It was time. How it was going to go from this point onwards was out of his hands. As the crowd clapped for the previous rider, he whispered to the heavens for Walter's help. The announcer came out onto the small stage at the side, it was the same man who just spoke to Katie. Katie was outside, knowing it was their turn, and started to hum her lullaby, Jan's ears flicked around to listen to her, Katie could feel Jan relax, the trust Jan had in Katie was on full display.

"It has come to my attention while outside just now, that number 16 this evening is a bit special, a horse I wasn't sure I'd ever see again until today, she has a rich history and I'm sure many will recognise her".

Roy looked at Neville with wide eyes. It was too late to change anything now. Everything he, Katie, and Jan had worked for came to this moment. Roy took a deep breath as the MC raised the microphone to speak again.

"Please welcome, 'For the Love of January', ridden this evening by Abigale Thompson".

Gage looked at his father as soon as they said the horse's name, then across the arena to see Katie looking regal in her Endeavour Park coat, sitting tall and proud coming into the arena. The crowd was completely silent. Roy sat on the edge of his chair, elbows on his knees, his hands over his mouth. He could barely breathe as she rode Jan out in front of everyone, stopping in front of the judges and gave an awkward salute. Katie bought Jan up into a gentle canter and lined her up for number 1. A single fence, Jan cleared it easily. Jumps 2, 3 and 4 were in the same line, set up as a triple, Jan turned her head to get a look at it, Katie with a slight wobble in saddle cleared them and onto number 5.

Gage didn't move an inch. He couldn't. He was terrified at what he was seeing. Nancy, with a smile so bright, watched with anticipation. With each jump, Roy moved further down his seat. Taylor kept looking back at Gage during Katie's set.

Katie came over 5,6, and 7 with no worries. Number 8 and 9 were starting to feel harder. The top Pole on number 9 wobbled but stayed. Roy hid his face. The final jump was a wall and the highest of the course. Katie looked at the final jump as she came around into line, Jan again turned her head to get a look before taking off, her back hoof just knocking the top as she went over, knocking the brick down. The crowd cheered loudly as she went over the last jump. Roy leapt to his feet and shook hands with Neville. Nancy and Belinda were emotional as they clapped loudly. Gage just stood there, he didn't clap, he didn't even crack the blank stare he had had the entire round. Neville and Roy excused themselves to find Katie.

Katie was standing against the practice yard fence with Lily, Jan tied off to the rail. Roy picked her up and spun her around.

"What a fucking awesome thing to watch", Roy could barely contain himself.

Katie was laughing, she was so happy. Lily hugged her father with excitement. Lily was proud of Katie; she understood the importance of Jan's performance and what it meant to her father. Katie checked her phone and sighed.

"I couldn't believe it, only one fault, you and Lily are both into the jump off."

The MC called a 30-minute intermission for riders to compose themselves before the jump off. Roy watched Katie check her phone again.

"I'm going to go sit back down with Mum," Roy said to Lily kissing her on the cheek. "Goodluck to you both".

Neville stayed with the girls to offer his great words of wisdom before the jump off round started.

Roy walked back into the arena. Gage wasn't sitting with the family anymore; he was nowhere to be seen. He walked through the waiting crowd to the dining room and Bar. Gage was sitting at the bar drinking a beer. Roy pulled out the bar stool beside Gage and sat down.

"They are about to start".

Gage stared ahead. Taking another mouthful of beer.

"You better get going then, wouldn't want to miss it". Gage's tone was icy cold and lacking any emotion.

"Gage", he touched his arm, Gage pulled away from the touch. "She's your girlfriend, she will want to look up and see you supporting her".

"Is she though, like is she really, all I see right now is a liar, she is just like Taylor," Gage held his beer up and drank the last mouthful before slamming the bottle down hard.

"Well buddy if you can't sit up there for Katie, at least sit there for your sister".

The MC announced the first 3 riders in the jump off. Two of them dropped a pole gaining faults on their scores and the third withdrew for unknown reasons. It came down to Lily and Katie. Lily was drawn out to ride next. Lily rode out onto the sand. Stopped and saluted the judges, looking up into the crowd to see her family. Lily rode clean until the final set of jumps. Her horse baulked suddenly sending Lily unexpectedly over the horse's head and into the sand. Gage stood up, hand over his mouth, she was ok, it was more hurt pride as she got back on her feet and waved to a cheering crowd. Neville took Lily's horse into the yard as Nancy watched from the sideline with her daughter and Gage as Katie was announced as the final rider. To win, they needed a clean round. Roy again sat nervously with Belinda in the stand. Jan seemed calm as Katie hummed to her. Saluting the judges she started her round. Jan turned her head on every jump, getting a good look at it with her good eye, it looked like each time she was going to go over partially sideways but at the last moment Jan would look forward again trusting Katie to guide her over safely. Katie turned the last corner and came onto the final jump. Roy stood up, his hands on his head, the nerves were almost debilitating as he closed his eyes, and in that moment, he saw Walter, watching with him, the world went into slow motion as he stood there in a never-ending pause of silence, his eyes still closed. Finally, the crowd erupted into loud cheers and clapping. Roy opened his tear-filled eyes. 'For the Love of January' had done it, she jumped a clear round.

Chapter 20

Just over a year later, Katie pulled her beloved Little Jim up in front of Endeavour Park and backed him into her spot beside the old, red float. Katie still lived at 'I Don't Give a Doo Dah'. She loved that little house, even the noisy ginger roommate that came with it, she wouldn't consider life anywhere else.

The morning air smelt like rain, and it was cold. Walking down the breezeway she could see her beloved Sterlo desperately trying to get her attention with his usual choir of nickering grunts. She pulled the handle to open his door into the outside pen, without hesitation he went out as a collection of snowflakes drifted down to rest neatly on his neck. Katie mucked out Sterlo's stable, pushing the wheelbarrow down the back path to the compost heap, looking off into the distance towards the paddock out on its own.

So much had happened at Endeavour Park since the day Jan jumped. The 5 furry vacuums, Katie's precious donkeys went to live at a Hobart Highschool as part of the agriculture program, their titles now, Emotional Support Donkeys, and man were they good at their jobs. Katie visited them there a few times, giving support to the school in ways of donations of food and to talk to the kids about the donkey's amazing purpose in their lives. After all, they do have a reputation for making hearts happy. Katie, Lily, and Gage had spent the last few days preparing for new additions to the family. Katie wrote names on the chalkboards above the stall doors.

A new collection of horses arrived later that morning. Neglected nags from an animal welfare case. 7 horses got off the truck. A massive brown and white Clydesdale, newly named Duke, moved into Stable 2 next to Sterlo, 2 little white mares named Faye and Ally went into 3 and 4, a stubby and moody Shetland pony named Coffey into 5, into 6 went an old grey pony named Winston and finally in 7 came Vegas, an appaloosa mare. The story would start again for Katie, just like it did when she first came to work at Endeavor Park with the riding school horses that were in these same stalls. All these horses were incredibly underweight, it was just the first chapter for them, it could only get better from here.

Taylor didn't make the Olympic Team which was probably a good thing for her mental health. Her journey after the trials ended on good terms with Gage and the family. She moved on to teach at an Equine college in Sydney which suited her. Gage wasn't sorry to see her go. Their history of on and off again relationships couldn't even really continue as friends.

'For the Love of January' and Katie made the national papers and the news. Katie sees the newspaper's front pages every time she walks the breezeway as she had them framed, hanging between each stable. It was perhaps, to her, the greatest achievement in her life.

'Hero horse's new life" one headline read. "A community's love for January" another said.

"Loving life remembered" is the one that hits hardest every time she glanced up at it, it's the one framed just before you walk out towards Jan's paddock. The last news story about 'For the Love of January' but for her the most important one.

Carrying a small posy of white flowers, Katie and Gage walked hand in hand along the tracks in the grass, down to the clearing with the two big trees. Katie let go of Gage's hand, walked forward to look at Clementine and Kota's headstones, digging deep into her pocket and pulling out a few pieces of carrot, Katie leant forward and placed them gently onto the top of the newest white cross amongst the tall, green, flower-filled grass. Snowflakes began to fall in an eerie silence, there was a special comforting sense that came with watching snow fall.

Tears fell from her eyes as she placed the flowers down in the grass, looking up and wiping her eyes, she knelt for a moment and read her name "For the Love of January". Some days, the pain of losing Jan was too much for her to handle. Her soul ached for Jan; Katie wasn't sure she would ever truly let her go. She was that once in a lifetime friend, a soulmate. She was special. Jan was a superstar. After Jan jumped in the showcase, Katie and Roy bought her home. Everyone wanted to see her, to know more about the beautiful, scarred girl who had come back to life the day she met Katie, so many people came for tours of Endeavour Park, just to see her. She became a Town icon.

It was only a few weeks later, early one rainy morning when Katie walked down the tracks in the grass, carrying Jan's halter ready for her morning training, humming the same beautiful lullaby she always sang to Jan. That morning nothing seemed abnormal, nothing out of place, but a part of Katie died when she stepped softly forward to the railing to find Jan that day. She was laying down, her head tucked neatly over her front leg, her beautiful eye closed just like she was sleeping, Katie called her, she didn't move, one foot at a time, she stepped through the railing and walked towards her, then she ran, ran harder than she had ever run before. She was gone. No explanation or cause of death could be found, she was just gone of natural causes. Katie barely remembered what happened after that. The sorrow that engulfed her body that day, and still comes back from time to time, was suffocating.

Katie found herself in Jan, and Jan found her life again in Katie. The bond they had was unbreakable. One journalist wrote that she had fulfilled her life's purpose and left to find Walter. Walter was the one who saved her, he loved her first, his love for her initially saved her life. Maybe animals, like humans, have a destiny, a life's purpose, the news story read, Jan's destiny was to jump but most of all it was to find Katie. Who knows why she was drawn to her paddock that first day at Endeavour Park, but she changed Katie's life. Somewhere, someone, something knew Katie needed to find 'The Love of January'.

In Thanks

This book is fiction, the general story, characters and plot etc were made up by me and are in no way a true story.

This book touches on Domestic Violence, if you or anyone you know are in need of help or just someone to talk to please call 1800RESPECT (1800737732). This service is free and 24/7. Please don't be scared to reach out for help, your story may just be one that saves someone else's life.

This book has been quite the adventure to write, it's part my imagination and contributions by others that truly made it come to life, there has been a number of people who have listened to what I had in mind and just added to the story's magic.

Thank you to Louise from The Lufra Hotel and Apartments in Eaglehawk Neck, Tasmania. I contacted her, over 12 months ago, randomly, via The Lufra Hotel's Facebook page in hope she may give me permission to use her establishment in my book. I'm sure she probably wondered WTF, is this a scam for a moment. She was absolutely amazing and agreed to talk to me on the phone, giving me local events and history, the info on the Doo-licous rentals in Dootown and info about her beautiful town that I could include in my story. She answered questions easily and probably thought I was a bit nuts at first, I'm sure, when talking to me. Thank you, Louise, I hope you enjoy reading the story.

Thank you to my horse loving work colleges at Petcare Extraordinaire, Guyong, Adina, Luke, and Jaimie who listened to my story ideas, especially Jaimie who helped me make the journey to Jan jumping. Your insight, listening to my ideas, and brainstorming over lunch breaks helped me bring Jan and her story to life and I can't thank you enough.

I am not completely sure if there actually is a Dootown cottage named "I Don't Give a Doo Dah", I couldn't find one with the name on an online search, but I could be wrong. If so, and there is a cottage with this name, your cottage name has played a big part in this story, thank you, the name started inspiring me when it came to the unique home I pictured in my mind while writing.

To Wendy, My amazing Publisher. Thank you for allowing me the freedom to be completely me when it comes to telling the stories. You are supportive, dedicated, and make it easy to express the vision, most importantly keeping the stories as Aussie as possible and for that I am forever grateful. You have never tried to change the way I tell my stories or the character's personalities and quirks in my books, the sometimes bogan way I describe things to me is what makes them like a yarn you would hear amongst friends or at the local pub over drinks...the type of story that changes with each person that retells it…. For me, the readers need to see and feel my take on the true blue Aussieness, I hope people feel when they read my stories, that is exactly what you give me every time, no questions.

Thank you to the readers. It's important to me, as I said before, to keep my stories as "Aussie" as I can. The Aussieness, the way we speak, think, and talk in my stories is what keeps them true to me and my sometimes-wacky way of telling a yarn. I dare say those close to me hear my voice when they read my stories, for that I am truly sorry, ha-ha.

This is book 3 of the Calendar Series, you, the readers, are what has kept my story ideas alive. I did not think people would appreciate shorter, more condensed Aussie type yarns and boy was I wrong. You readers are what make the stories truly come alive, your messages to my social media pages about my books and how much you have enjoyed the stories mean more to me than I could ever express...Thank you so much for investing in my story telling. Can't wait to share the next adventure with you all.

More Stories by Jackie Clark

The Calendar Series: Available in print and eBook formats

Book 1: November

Book 2: The December Rains

Other Books

The Little Things: Things to know, before I go.

(Available in print format only)